Awakened

A Global Paranormal Security Agency Story

Jodi Kendrick

SoulGate Publishing

The Global Paranormal Security Agency

The Global Paranormal Security Agency is a hidden investigative group dedicated to bridging the paranormal and human worlds in an effort to keep everyone safe.

Protect. Defend. Seek Justice.

Thank you!
To my family, friends and writing community. Your continued love, support and encouragement keep me going. Without you, I'd still be dabbling and drifting.

Jessica Ripley – So many projects to keep me out of trouble!

To **Milly Taiden** – my deep appreciation for her generosity in opening her creative worlds to those of us that enjoyed playing in them.

For my Family.

ONE

AT NINE A.M. AGENT Carson Parenga wandered into the Director's office, coffee in hand, greeting fellow agents he knew and politely acknowledging new faces. The red-eye flight from his little island had him jet-lagged and bleary eyed, but Maeda had been insistent over the phone when he called him to come in. His gaze drifted over his Global Paranormal Security Agency colleagues.

Jack Maeda handed Carson a beige file folder. "Agent Ortega called us, asked for you specifically. Two victims, their bodies mutilated and left on the beach. A local pawn shop owner and a spiritual leader of the downtrodden. Seems the good minister works with the vulnerable population."

"Mutilated how?" It was too damned early for this conversation. Carson sipped his coffee. From the corner of his eye, he caught Willow staring at his cup, longing clear on her face before she turned to talk to an unknown redhead. That must be Olivia, the new recruit.

"Bite marks from some large creature. But there's also a symbol carved into the back of the victim's heads. Locals can't decide between a cult or a rabid animal of the large kind."

Definitely too early. "Great."

"Next flight's at one."

Carson sighed.

Chase and Kai leaned in to peek at the crime scene photo half out of the folder. "Better you than us, man," Kai said.

"Thanks."

Carson's attention was drawn to Mike and Risa, at the mention of Back Water Bay and Ursanis. Risa was selling Willow on their mission to the arctic.

"Aww, damn, I'll trade you!" Carson grinned.

Willow quickly shot down the offer.

"I always get the messy cases. I'm considering retirement."

Director Maeda glanced up at Carson, "Not yet, old man, you still have plenty of work to do."

"Old man? What are you, thirty? Thirty-five?" Kai asked him.

"Something like that."

Maeda snorted.

CARSON STEPPED INTO THE sun-warmed water tumbling over his feet. The firm beach sand fell away as the surf sucked it back toward the ocean, luring him. Fiberglass board in hand, he tipped it forward and launched himself over the surface of the water, riding toward the ocean haze beyond the edge of the pier. As the sea paused and began its inward press, his powerful arms worked through it, keeping the surfboard from being pushed back, just until it shifted again, luring him farther out.

After several intense days reviewing the case, Ortega had suggested a swim, recommending this location for its waves. Driving from the precinct to the beach, the thirty second news break on the radio had recapped the day's progress. Journalist's wife wanted as a suspect in her husband's disappearance, police looking for the public's help in locating her. Second body found on beach, some locals fear large wild animal while others suspect a rise in local cult activities. Small congregation mourn the loss of their spiritual leader, a vigil will be held later in the evening. Still no word on the twelve young women and two young men gone missing from the community and surrounding areas along the coast. Politicians going head to head over funding cuts and gas prices again on the rise.

He needed the peace.

The farther the ocean pulled him out, the faster the responsibilities of the world rolled off his shoulders, until all he could hear was the roar of the surf and the cry of the seagulls riding the winds over head.

This case wasn't going to be a light beach walk. He floated for a long time beyond the end of the pier, the water tugging on the tether attaching the surf board to his ankle. It was the last irritant of the land world to be shed. Feeling secure that he was far enough out of sight of land to be forgotten by any beach bystander, he unfastened the ankle strap and instead tied it to a chain strung around one of the thick posts supporting the pier.

The seagull that had been keeping pace with him cried out, and he let himself drop down below the surface, ignoring the power of the surf rushing around the pier supports. Anchoring a foot against the post, he pushed himself farther out to sea, catching the current.

Then he shifted. The water around him rippled as his energy writhed through the ocean water. A moment later, Carson no longer existed. In his place floated a large, clawed, reptilian creature.

With a swish of his powerful tail, he was much farther out to sea than he could have ever paddled in human form. Muscles bunched and released in another surge out into the depths of the water, away from humanity and its complexities.

He needed to think.

Ana had been right to call him in.

His grief and frustration slid away with the fathoms. Faces of mangled victims dissipated as the ocean cleansed them from his memory—for a time. The simplicity of predator-prey cycled through him. Not the same as the predator-prey of humanity; doing evil things not for subsistence, but for self-pleasure and gain. Nothing to do with survival, and everything to do with games of power and control.

Pushing hard through the water, diving deeper, seeking the silence of the deepest parts of the ocean.

Deeper still as the pressure encased him. Leveling out the dive, and sliding along, seeking.

Seeking what?

He stopped pushing through the water and floated. Thoughts drifted through his mind; he just let them tumble as he remained suspended in the cold darkness of the ocean. Letting the energy of the ocean work its way over his thick scale-covered skin, seeping into his pores, pushing the trauma and stress out of his being. An osmosis: Release the depravity of humanity, intake the simplicity of the sea, like tidal surges scrubbing him clean.

Goddess?

After a long moment, with nothing but silence shifting around him, he projected the question outward. Once, and then once more as a mental roar. Would she hear him, wherever she may be? She hadn't answered in a very long time.

He was tired after centuries of guardianship over the humans. Despite looking to be in his mid-thirties, the director referred to him as 'old man' and ribbed him about retirement for a reason. In the moment, the idea was very appealing.

He wanted to 'retire' as his director, Jack Maeda, would say.

He drifted over a region of underwater caves, 'listening' in barely suppressed desperation for the Goddess' energy signature.

He felt nothing.

Whether slumbering or awake, she was not anywhere near this aqua-territory.

After a few hours, he made his way back toward the surfboard attached to the pier, his mind clearer after the swim.

AN ELECTRIC SCENT DRIFTED past Lirikai's nostrils as the current eddied around her. Tugging, enticing her from the blackness of her cave.

The scent of power.

Curiosity encouraged awareness. Other scents had tried to pull her from her deep dormancy over the centuries but were never enough to awaken her. Not fully.

This scent wasn't the appetizing scent of prey that teased her hunger. For a long time, she ignored it. This was different, and yet familiar.

In her human form, it would have been like a deeply forgotten scent attached to a vital memory. A particular meadow or seaside location where a life changing event occurred.

It curled through the current sliding over her fins and scales, wrapping itself around her. Flexing the muscles of her body, the water slid under the edges of the razor-edged scales like silk over bared flesh, making it thrum.

Lured, her fins began working, her tail weaving through the water, propelling her toward the mouth of the cave.

She followed the trail, and more scents encircled her. Then the vibrations of the ocean worked their way through her layers. Slowly, she acclimated, moving as though tethered to the drifting scent of power that had captured her attention.

As sleep fell away, coherent thought filled the space despite the fog of deep ocean pressure.

What was calling her?

How much time had passed?

Had the Goddess also awakened from her slumber so much longer than her own?

Did any of her sisters still exist? Had they survived the centuries?

On emerging from the cave, she began to drift toward the lightness of the surface, tasting, smelling, feeling the ocean along the way.

She ignored the urge to sink back into the darkness of the cave.

Her senses were assaulted by alien scents and vibrations. The ocean felt wrong, tainted, sick.

Through it, the thread of that enticing scent tickled her dorsal fin, teasing, promising something worthwhile if she just followed along.

Curiosity drew her out and set her course.

Other, more familiar scents began to work their way through the ocean water, awakening the hunger.

Hunger, she knew. And a feast she could smell.

Her lithe body moved through the currents like a silver flash of lightening following a branch to its filament.

Curiosity and delicious hunger.

TWO

LIRIKAI FOLLOWED THE SCENT to shore. The power signature drifted in and out of massive pier posts. She was so close to shore, the power of the surf enticed her toward the beach.

Hunger overrode control and curiosity, especially now that the trail seemed to end here. Too many years without indulging in a hunt and she could feel the urge to frenzy creeping over her.

She drifted back and away beyond the catch of the pier, vying for control and coherent thought.

Enough!

She snapped her powerful jaws in irritation, and the protruding uneven spears of teeth vibrated from the impact and rippled back up into her skull.

She needed to feed on something before following the delicious scent that called to her. After a moment more, she turned back to deeper ocean to fill her belly.

And to figure out if she remembered her human form enough to reshape herself.

Her jaws closed over several unwary fish. She swallowed, oblivious to their frantic flipping and twisting to escape. Memory of the shape and feel of legs and arms formed in her mind. *Ah yes.*

Hair, ears, breasts, fingers and toes.

Another swallow of wriggling fish.

Clothing.

A memory of one of the last times she emerged and the frenzy of the villagers that followed. Half had thought her a water demon luring their men away for wanton endeavors. The other half dropped to her feet enthralled naming her their water goddess.

Not quite right on both accounts, but not too far off the mark on both accounts, either.

She was a servant of the Goddess and yet a demon to those inciting her wrath.

In the end, that last time, she had eaten a couple of humans from both camps. Work done, she returned to the ocean.

Showing up naked on shore never began the relationship with the right tone.

She floated a while longer, her fins and tail waving in the current.

There was no sign of the Goddess, no call, no signal, no trace. Only the tingle of power.

Power enough to awaken her from centuries of slumber. She still hadn't been able to re-call what was familiar about the signature, but there was something. She hadn't found the right nerve yet. It was just at the edge of her skull, tickling the senses along her bones. She wriggled, trying to dispel the sensation and re-turn her focus to the nearby beach.

Right now, she had to recall her human form, and do her duty hunting the delicious scent of predator-prey. The savoury taste of one that would inflict terrible deeds on another for no purpose but to find pleasure in it. They were the ones that tasted the best.

With a flick of her head, her jaw caught an-other cluster of passing fish from their school.

This was what the Goddess had created her for—created her, and her sisters, to do. The Goddess would answer the prayers of her fol-lowers, and the Barra'kidai would seek her vengeance, rewarded with the tastiest of vil-lains.

If she were in her human form, she would be nigh on drooling.

With a surge, she threw herself into the wave rushing toward the beach, and with the right mental concentration, rolled out of the surf and over the pasty sand with shapely limbs, and soft flesh rosy with the glow of the setting sun.

The beach wasn't abandoned, but nearly so at this time of day. She remained as she was, collecting the muscle memory required to move the gangly limbs in the right way to get her up and moving away from the ocean.

The dimming light masked her nudity, as she found her footing and moved back toward the shelter of the pier to get a sense of what was around her, and the most effective source of clothing.

It didn't take long for a retreating family to drop a towel unnoticed. Once they were far enough away, she awkwardly ran out to grab it and returned to the shadows of the pier supports before one of the humans returned to the area realizing they'd left something behind.

Hidden, she observed the humans. Their clothes, their manner, the buildings along the road above the beach.

From this distance, she could see that the world had changed a great deal while she slept. Far more than it usually did.

Wrapping the thick linen securely around herself, she stepped out from the shelter of the pier, and moved purposefully toward the humanity at the other side of the beach shelf.

That power signature was out here somewhere.

And there would be plenty of food to sustain her between then and now. She could taste them in the air already.

Her mouth did indeed water.

CARSON PULLED THE LAST strap, securing his surfboard set in the back of his jeep. The wind was picking up, and he didn't want to lose his favourite board. He'd gone through the effort of checking it through 'oversized' luggage through two airports.

Parked in the sandy lot above the beach, he was tempted to go back out, for just a little longer. He stood a moment, feeling the tug, watching the waves, when he noticed a figure roll out of the surf and unsteadily make for the shelter of the pier supports.

Pulled back to the rolling ocean, he dropped his keys into the pocket of his cargo shorts, disengaged his feet from his flip-flops and let his feet dig into the sand one step at a time.

The call of a mother to her teenage son about a forgotten towel, and his reply that he couldn't find it, drifted over the rising wind and hush of each wave coming faster.

"... It isn't there, Ma."

The mother's disbelieving voice chattered about selective obliviousness and stomped over to where the family had been set up.

He smirked when she came away empty handed. One for the kid. A win for all kids around the globe, hearts rejoicing.

By now his toes were caked with wet sand, anticipating the flutter of water that would encase them. Once achieved, he turned and strolled in the direction of the pier. Maybe that elusive towel had been blown in that direction, although he didn't think the wind was quite strong enough for that yet.

Moving closer to the shadowy space, his pace slowed as he squinted into the shaded area. His instincts tugged at his skin and the hair on his arms and scalp rose.

He stopped as though taking a moment to watch the sea again and made a quick surveillance of the beach. By now, with the incoming storm, it was nearly abandoned.

Turning his attention back in the direction of the pier, his body jerked upon seeing a figure standing several dozen feet away. He blinked. It was a woman, wrapped in a beach towel. Her wet hair clung to her shoulders, and her eyes were glued to him.

His instincts sang louder, coursing the blood through his body faster.

The figure that rolled out of the surf?

Was she the one he'd been hunting?

They stared at each other across the distance. He drew in a breath and stepped forward, body taut. "May I be of assistance, Ma'am?"

Her head tilted back as she stepped toward him. She looked as though she were scenting the air.

His body tensed, ready in case she proved to be more of a threat than she appeared to be. As a non-human, he knew better.

She was close enough now he could see the smile spread on her lips. Clouds scudded across the sky, billowed by the storm winds. The rising moon illuminated her, and his breath fled.

The moon silvered her near-translucent flesh; ocean beads glimmered along her limbs and ends of her hair. Her curvy body seemed to be naked beneath the beach towel which covered her torso and hips, but left her lean legs visible for appreciation. She had full lips, a small nose, and incredibly pale eyes with unusual pupils that marked her as not truly human.

Her voice, when she spoke, was a soft rasp and the words were in a language he'd not heard in centuries.

She frowned when he failed to answer.

"Goddess?"

He remembered that word. Finding the mobility, he inclined his head, searching for the forgotten words to respond, letting her make the approach. He still didn't know what her intent was.

And if she was old enough to communicate in this language, Goddess on her lips, he couldn't predict anything. Except maybe trouble.

This wasn't how he'd envisioned ending his long, long week.

THREE

LIRIKAI STARED AT THE man, sensing his mind at work. She could smell the Goddess on him, and the sea. She was sure this was the scent that had awakened her from her dark cave.

She stepped closer. "Who are you?"

Why was he here?

Why had she been compelled to follow him?

She stepped closer still. He tensed.

She frowned at his wariness.

"Goddess?"

A thrill swept through her at his expression. He was adorable as confused recognition swept over him. She watched him struggle for words. He inclined his head.

"It's been so long since I have spoken to another soul, let alone another of the Goddess' blessings," she said with another step.

His hand came up, as though to hold her at bay. Haltingly, he said, "I struggle to recall the ancient language."

She nodded. She'd been asleep so long, she struggled to recall speech at all. It had been so long since she'd assumed human form.

His gaze studied her form. "You need clothing."

Looking more closely at what he was wearing, her hand moved to the thick linen she'd wrapped around herself. "Yes".

The wind gusted harder, flattening the linen against her body, teasing the edge from unraveling around her.

"Come?" he held a hand out to her. "My car is close."

She didn't take his hand, but smiled, and gestured for him to lead the way to wherever he was proposing they go.

On reaching the level ground above the beach, she hesitated.

He offered her the spare footwear he'd left in the sand, then rummaged for spare clothing in the back of a large metal cart of sorts. The clothing was like what he was wearing, and she donned them while he waited with his back turned.

He opened the door for her, let her step in and settle on the seat, then closed it and headed around to the driver's side.

Showing her the seatbelt, she mimicked him.

As soon as he started the engine, and pulled out onto the road, her right hand gripped the bar attached to the door beside her, but she remained otherwise impassive.

Inside, her mind was racing. She barely remembered the English she'd learned the last time she was awake in the world, and it certainly didn't sound like what little she heard now.

And this wagon! Incredible! She wondered if it could go faster than the light sailing ships she and her sisters used to race.

The roads were smooth, and they moved quickly through the city. She took it all in. The buildings, the shops, how people were dressed, snippets of exchange, music. Oh, the music! Everything had changed so much while she slept.

FOUR

CARSON LED THE WOMAN into the station. During the ride, he'd watched her from the corner of his eye. She took everything in. Flinched at nothing, following.

She said it had been a long time since she'd spoken to anyone. How long?

What was she? Not human.

He thought he knew what she was, or at least a strong suspicion. But he couldn't be sure.

Even now, she observed everything around her, taking it all in.

Was she somehow connected to the case he'd been called in for? He'd gone to the ocean to meditate, and this woman had mysteriously appeared on the beach.

He shot her another glance, ensuring she still followed him.

He knew looks meant nothing when it came to predators. Especially if she was a child of the Goddess.

He had to get her to Analiese Ortega's office for assessment and integration with the Global Paranormal Security Agency if it turned out to be necessary.

Wading through the press of noise and bodies in the bullpen toward the quiet of the office doors at the back of the room, he glanced again to check that she still cared to follow him, despite knowing nothing of where they were going or why.

She wasn't directly behind him.

She stood in the center of the room. His shirt and shorts hung loose on her, but she held herself as though she were a sea goddess. His mind conjured the image of her in a peplos. The noise dimmed somewhat as several men stopped talking to stare at her. Her eyes slid from person to person, body tense, nostrils twitching almost imperceptibly.

Something wasn't right, Carson moved toward her as her eyes silvered, pupils shifting to slits.

He reached for her. The expression on her face as he stepped into her sphere would have terrified a lesser being. He could feel his scales threatening to erupt over his skin in self-protection. Despite that, he stepped in close, blocking her view of the others in the room.

She blinked, nostrils flaring. Her eyes changed from wild and alien back to normal human eyes.

"Are you alright?" He asked in the old tongue.

She nodded, leaning toward him, inhaling. "They make me very hungry."

Hungry?

"I'll get you food."

She turned her head to the left, licking her lips. "That one smells tasty."

He followed her line of sight. "No, no, uhm, you don't want that one." He slipped his hand around hers and drew her back toward the office door. "Come this way, I'll get you food," he promised. He was going to have to call Jack. The director would want to hear all about this new discovery.

She resisted the tug of his hand, leaning toward another perp, "This one will do."

He pulled her, lightening fast, in through the door and slammed it shut. "You can't eat them." He said.

"Why not? They smell delicious, they're perfect."

"Excuse me?" a voice floated toward them from behind the large desk.

"Analiese, Hi, this is..." he turned his question to the woman, speaking in the old tongue, "What are you called?"

"Lirikai."

"She mentioned the Goddess," he said in English to Ana.

"Oh?"

He heard Ana's chair scrape the floor, her footsteps brought her close. "Lirikai?"

At the call of her name, she turned her attention to Ana, who smiled at her, but she remained mute.

"How may we help you, Lirikai?"

"Help?" Lirikai repeated, "Wake. Hungry... . Now," she said in broken English.

Ana's eyes slid to Carson and back to Lirikai, "What do you eat?"

"Eat..." There was a long pause as Lirikai searched for words. "Human food, but bad people taste best." she turned her head back toward the door, licking her lips again with longing.

"I see, won't you sit?" Ana's hand swept toward the chairs placed in front of her desk, then walked around back toward her own seat, lifted the handset of the phone and poked a pre-set number "Freddie, grab the most palatable food from the cafeteria...ASAP," she added, her eyes lifted back to Lirikai, as she retrieved her seat and replaced the phone.

Carson waited for Lirikai to sit, then took the other chair, between her and the door, stretching out his long legs to fill the space. "I found her on the beach about half an hour ago."

Ana's brows shot up, "Fast work, Carson."

He shrugged, "She rolled out of the ocean, no clothes, speaking the ancient language and asking about the Goddess. Thought she might need your handy dandy 'Assessment and Integration' skills."

"You think she might be tied to your case?"

"Sometimes the Goddess delivers in strange ways. Most often not and it's just coincidence. In this case?" He shrugged again, "Gut says she is."

Ana reached into one of her desk drawers, and placed a digital recorder on her desk, switching it on.

"Lirikai," Ana said, drawing the woman's attention back to her.

Lirikai had been looking at the room decor, seemingly unengaged. At the sound of her name, her eyes snapped back to Ana.

"Are you comfortable communicating in English?"

"English different now."

"We can make do, the old language is coming back to me, ask what you want to know, and we'll sort it out," Carson said.

"Why did you bring me here?" Lirikai suddenly asked Carson in the old tongue.

"You indicated you'd been away a long time. I'm a member of the Global Paranormal Security Agency. We—Ana can help you adjust to the world. A lot has changed."

"I can go back to the sea."

"What brought you here?" he asked her, something pulled at him.

Carson could have asked her all this earlier, but his instinct had been to bring her in to see Ana, who listened without interruption, despite their conversing in the old language. He'd review the recording with her later.

"You did."

Carson's lips twitched."You came out of the ocean?"

She nodded."Why?"

"You."

This time he frowned. "Explain."

"I slept a very long time, in a cave along the ocean floor. Your scent drifted into my cave. You smell of the Goddess, and something else—I'm not sure what. I followed the trail."

Carson suppressed a thrill. Was she a mermaid? He considered his next questions. "When were you last awake?"

She didn't answer right away. A frown pulled at her forehead before she answered, "Centuries, I think. I can't be sure."

"Centuries!" he said in English, his gaze drifting to Ana. Quickly returning to the old language, "But why?"

Lirikai dropped her gaze to her hands. The moment dragged out. When she answered, her voice was tight, "I was alone. The Goddess was gone for a very long time. My sisters were disappearing. Some were finding mates and returning to life on land. Others were killed in battles. Too many killed." Her fingers clasped together. She looked up, her gaze steady on his face, despite the unexpressed sorrow in her eyes.

"I'm sorry," he whispered.

There was a brisk knock on the door before it jerked open. A young man stepped in carrying a tray of food that he dropped on Ana's desk with a clatter, then rushed back out of the room, jerking the door closed again.

Lirikai eyed the food. "Why won't you let me take one of them?" she jerked her head toward the door. "There are so many. I'll take him to the ocean, no mess."

Carson hastily grabbed the tray, depositing it on her thighs. "We don't eat perpetrators. At least not anymore." He said in English, then added "That's why you're here. So, we can integrate you into modern society."

"Or I could just return to the ocean and not bother," she lifted the plastic spoon frowning at the food that dropped from it, splattering back onto the plate. "This is edible?"

"Usually."

She sighed, took a bite and swallowed. She looked as though she were in pain. She dropped the spoon, "I'd rather eat more fish." She started to rise, but Carson extended his hand to take the tray back and quickly placed it back on the desk.

Ana reached out with a finger, pushing the tray as far to the edge of the desk as possible without it falling over. "Why do you want to eat the people in the other room?"

"That's what we do. The Goddess created us to devour the vilest among us." She answered in the old language, and Carson translated, the words coming more naturally now.

"How could you know who is who?" Ana asked her, reaching for her notepad and pen.

"I smell them. The viler their intentions and deeds, the more delicious they smell and taste."

Ana's face paled when Carson relayed Lirikai's response.

"Do you eat all of them? When was the last time you... ate someone?" Carson asked, rising from his chair and looking out of the office window into the bullpen.

"We don't eat the heads, they are for the Goddess. Not in a very long time," She sighed, they all heard her stomach growl as she licked her lips again.

"Not the heads." Carson's voice was low, he rubbed a hand over his face. He turned to look down at Lirikai. "Would you tell me if you had eaten someone recently?"

She shrugged, unconcerned with the question. "If I had, the scent drifting in from the other room would not be making me salivate so much. You did not tell me why eating the guilty is not permitted. It is my right to feed. The Goddess created me for this purpose."

"You said you went to sleep because the Goddess had gone away for a long time?" he waited for her nod. "I have been around a long time too, and have not felt the Goddess' presence since soon after I was created. Either she's gone or she is dormant, like you were. Her power no longer rules here. We now live by the rule of law—Human law, which does not permit cannibalism."

Lirikai got to her feet. "I am not a cannibal. I do not eat my own kind."

Carson's hands went up in a placating gesture, which didn't seem to calm her at all.

"Move, I wish to leave."

"You must understand, the world is different. You may not eat humans."

"I will eat whom I please," her voice rolled toward him.

Lowering his hands, he braced his feet, planting himself firmly between Lirikai and the door. He heard Ana's seat shift as she pushed herself back toward the wall.

"Just because your scent roused me from slumber, does not mean I will be subservient to your wishes, youngling."

Youngling? He nearly laughed but had enough self-preservation not to. She was indeed far more ancient than he was, but he still didn't know exactly what she was or how dangerous she could be. Given that she was created in the time before he was and had been dormant for who-knew how many centuries, he wouldn't push her too hard until he knew more about her. He wouldn't risk Ana's life, or the lives of those in the next room.

The longer he blocked her path, the angrier she became. The energy rippled toward him, and he could feel his scales forming. Her eyes had gone to slits again, and this time she opened her mouth, large teeth began to grow and elongate from the delicate perimeter of her lovely mouth.

The door jerked open again behind him, "Jesus!" Freddie squeaked, slamming the door closed again.

"Who?" Lirikai demanded.

Carson kept his eyes on Lirikai.

"Move."

He shook his head.

Lirikai growled, stepping forward.

Ana's phone rang, startling Lirikai. She snapped it up, "What?" After a moment, she put the phone down again. "Freddie said they found another one, Carson."

"Shit." He ran a hand over his forehead, eyes still glued to Lirikai's angry face. He thought quickly on what she'd told them, eyes lingering on her teeth. "You said about the heads, that 'they are for the Goddess'."

She didn't move.

"Would you help me?" He forced his body into a less defensive posture, gambling.

Curiosity flashed in her eyes as they returned to their human color.

He waited another moment.

Her teeth receded and she looked fully human again. Ana's sigh of relief spoke for both of them.

"I'm here to work on a murder case... it involves heads and unusual bite marks."

The corner of her mouth went up, "If I help you, do I get to-"

"No," he cut in quickly, "But I know a great steak place—steak is beef."

She pulled a face.

"Trust me. It's the best."

Suspicion warred with her earlier curiosity, though finally she nodded.

He glanced at Ana, who sagged in her chair. He blew out a breath. "Shall we go have a look at my work station?"

Lirikai picked up the abandoned tray and jammed several spoonfuls of the mystery food into her mouth, washing it all down with the entire cup of water. "Your cook should be eaten for that slop."

Her eyes twinkled and he laughed.

FIVE

LIRIKAI FOLLOWED CARSON BACK through the open area, doing her very best to ignore the aroma of the exploiters, rapists and murderers. They all smelled so good. But she had decided to help him, and it seemed eating the guilty was now forbidden.

Maybe later, she would hunt and lure one away. He would never know. There would be nothing left for anyone to find. As it should be.

So, with curiosity, she followed him into another room, smaller than the one belonging to his colleague Ana, but this one was far less clean. There were stacks of documents everywhere and images stuck to the walls and windows. Her hand reached for a stack, her fingers sliding over the surface of it. So smooth and fine.

"It's not that file," Carson said over his shoulder, then turned and handed her a similar one.

She held it across her upturned palms, unsure what to do with it. With care, she balanced the items on one hand, and lifted the top leaf. "What is this?"

He gave her a blank look, "It's a case file. Oh-Jesus, I forgot. Can you read?"

Lirikai looked down at the pages. The lines of script just that. She didn't recognize the characters. "Not this."

He ran a hand through his hair, snatched the folder up from her hands and smacked it down on top of the stack on his desk, "Here," he said, flipping it open. Her heart bounced up in to her throat at how carelessly he handled such precious materials.

Snapping several sheets over, he spread out several with images on them. She gasped. They were so lifelike! She looked up at him; he stared back at her expectantly. "Incredible," she breathed, hesitant to touch it.

Carson jabbed a blunt finger on the surface, "This— do you know this?"

Her eyes slid to where he pointed.

The image was of a mangled man, puncture parks on random parts of the headless body.

"Sloppy," she said.

"Sloppy?" he took a step back.

"Messy and wasteful, if he was a bad man."

"And if he wasn't?" Carson's voice took on an odd tone.

"Then unfortunate, and he should be mourned by his people."

"I see."

Lirikai squinted at the bite marks. "Why would you waste your vellum on such images? Wouldn't art be a better investment?"

"Vellum? The paper? It's easily made and cheap now," he said, pushing through several other sheets, "What of this one?"

She was taken aback by his dismissive attitude but turned her attention to the new image he pointed at.

There it was.

Her breath locked in her throat, and her stomach flipped.

The head, or rather the back of a very roughly detached head. It was inelegant. Whoever had done the detaching had struggled, but the lower part of the back of the head, where the skull meets the spine, had the hair shaved away to make room for a symbol carved into the flesh.

The door jerked open, the one called Freddie popped his head into the room, eyes widening when he saw Lirikai. His gaze shot to Carson,

"Got a location on the new body, boss wants to know when you're going?"

"Now."

Freddie disappeared again.

"Does he always do that?" "Yep," he said, sliding his documents together again, and tucking the lot under his arm, then motioning her toward the door. "Let's go."

Carson snapped a colored paper from Freddie's extended hand as they made their way back through the crowded area toward the exit.

"Car is this way," he said, walking through the open space of other cars of varying shapes and sizes. She climbed in while he tucked the sheets into a pocket attached to the back of his seat. While he situated himself, she looked around at the buildings, the lanterns, the sounds and smells of the air. Everything was so different. It truly was another world she had awakened to.

Could she adjust this time? Did she want to? There had always been changes to adapt to on awakening from a hibernation. But this one had been the longest in her lifetime.

She could always return to the sea. For now, Lirikai would make the most of this new era. She watched Carson closely as he made the car come alive and drove them out onto the road. Clearly, he'd adapted. She could too, if she chose to stay land-side.

If.

If she had a reason to. Her gaze swept Carson's profile, admiring his clean features, the nicely defined muscles under his shirt and his long legs. Away from the bustle of the crowded building, she could feel the undertone of his energy sweeping over her aura. She closed her eyes, reveling in the sensations of the wind on her face and hair, and his aura mingling with hers.

"What do you make of the pictures?"

She opened her eyes. "The body and head?" She shrugged, although he hadn't taken his gaze from the road ahead of them. "What happens to the person that did these things?"

"We will catch them. Then interrogate them to understand what happened and why, then imprison them."

"This is the human way?"

"For the most part, yes. But if this is one of our people - like you and me, as I suspect it is, then we must try to compromise between human law, and our own ways." They came to a stop and he turned his gaze on her. "The world is a very different place now, Lirikai. Our world, everything changed while you were sleeping." His expression was one of concern as he regarded her.

They were moving again, and he turned his eyes back to the road. Her stomach twisted at the loss of his attention.

The smell of the sea grew stronger. They turned onto a road that ran parallel to the ocean, traveling for what seemed to her to be a long distance. The landscape flew past them, as though she swam at her full speed. The moon illuminated the water rippling in the distance, hills and trees rolled past. Other cars intermittently blinded her with their lights, and they whipped past them. She closed her eyes, lulled by the motion of the car.

Her eyes snapped open when the car slowed and began bouncing over rough terrain. Sitting up from her slouched position, Carson smiled at her. "We're here. Maybe you'll solve this for us, and we can all go home, case closed."

They left the car on a rise overlooking a small bay, then picked their way down the rocky slope toward a brightly lit portion of rocky beach. It looked to her as though the sun had been stuffed into a large tent. People moved in and out of it, covered head to toe in white.

She glanced down at herself. Would Carson's borrowed clothing be acceptable for this ritual? He was dressed much like she was, and he seemed unconcerned.

She squinted against the square lanterns pointed at the tent. Someone broke from the group as they approached. Carson pulled something from his pocket, holding it up to the newcomer, who removed their head and face covering.

"Lana."

"Carson. Who's your friend?"

"Lirikai."

The woman's eyebrow raised.

Carson gestured toward the tent, "Same as the others?"

She nodded. "Suit up." She led the way to an area that had more white suits like her own.

Carson put one on, indicating that Lirikai should do the same.

She felt as though she were carefully wrapped in a shroud with almost nothing of herself exposed to the world. When it came time to pull the head and face coverings on, she hesitated, and only relented when the woman, Lana, insisted. Lirikai was constantly pulling at one section or another of the suit.

"You get used to it." Carson said as they were about to step into the illuminated tent. "Don't touch anything."

Inside, everything was too close. Lirikai focused on the sound of the ocean. It wasn't like her comfortable little cave where the sea flowed in and out. This tiny space didn't have a rhythm. It was a slice of the world blocked out.

What was she doing here? Just a few short hours ago, she'd been contentedly slumbering, oblivious to the world. But here she was, wrapped up in a tent to stare at someone's leavings.

The body itself had ragged crescents impressed into it, the skin broken and punctured. The head had been roughly detached. Hair and blood sprinkled the sand and the remains.

Despite the face covering, the scent of blood invaded her nostrils, and with it the underlying aroma of a guilty soul. It was nearly gone now, as the body had cooled after death. It was like staring at a fisherman's offal pile. And yet her gaze was glued to the corpse. The urge to bite made her mouth tingle, but it wasn't as overwhelming as it had been back at Carson's work building.

It looked like a poor example of Barra'kidai work - a sister? An impostor? She was sure that if someone turned the head over, there would be a shaved patch with a symbol carved into it too. Like in Carson's paper images. A token for the Goddess. But at the same time, this wasn't how it was supposed to be. None of this should be here. Justice was supposed to be exacted in the sea. The land wasn't the domain of the Barra'kidai. They were creatures of the sea goddess. The guilty were taken to their end in the ocean, to no longer be a blight on the world. The exposed bite marks read like frenzied desperation. The ritual was befouled.

She suddenly felt as though her shroud were constricting and crawling over her. The waves crashing in the surf called to her.

"Lirikai?" Carson called after her as she shoved her way outside, tearing the white barrier from her skin, eyes on the nearby ocean. She dropped the suit on the sand. Carson caught up to her, stripping off his own suit, leaving it with hers. He reached for her arm, "What do you know?"

She was forced to turn toward him when his strong grip halted her escape. Looking down at his hand encircling her arm, her anger rose sudden and hot. "Release me."

His fingers jerked open, but he remained insistent, leaning toward her as he spoke, "You know what happened to the victim."

"I am done here. I'm going back to the sea."

"I need to know what is happening here, Lirikai. If this killing is being done by one of ours, I must follow the law and handle it. My job is to protect the humans from those of our kind that can't co-exist." He dropped his voice so that it didn't carry back to the crew surrounding the tent.

The wind shifted, washing the scent of his power over her, enticing her toward him. The scent that had awakened and beckoned her from her hibernation.

His gaze was locked on her face, and the moment she relented, his intent expression relaxed, "Come on, let's get something to eat."

Her eyes drifted to the tent.

"Human food."

"I don't want more human food if the world now thinks that offal you gave me earlier is what is good."

Carson laughed, "Cafeteria food is always the worst. I promised you steak, but at this time of night, we'll have to settle for burgers instead."

She shrugged, falling in step next to him.

They climbed the rise to where his cart was parked. "What is cafeteria?"

Opening the door, he smiled, "The goddess' joke on us for straying too far out of the ocean and for too long."

SIX

CARSON COULD BARELY CONTAIN his excitement. She knew something.

Lirikai had knowledge that could help him stop the perpetrator, close the case, and return home.

He'd been called in on the case because of the unusual bite marks. The ritual marking might not have stood out as 'other' on its own, but both together did. The locals feared an out-of-control cult.

FBI had contacted GPSA, who disrupted his peaceful life on his little island. Peaceful, if not a little lonely. He'd agreed to work the case when the director called him, and had regretted it as soon as he read the case files during the flight west.

Glancing at the dash clock, he saw just how late it was getting. Lana had promised that her team liaison would send him the new data in the morning, and they still had a long drive back. His stomach rumbled, reminding him of his repeated promises of food for Lirikai.

He turned off the main highway, looking for an illuminated burger joint sign.

Once Carson ordered various items from the menu, they settled in at a large table farthest from the counter and door so they couldn't be overheard. Even at this hour, there were a few other patrons loitering, some biding time until they had to find a corner to sleep, others avoiding their spouses, and a couple were making deals. Making note of their positions, he settled in so that he could keep an eye on anyone that might take an interest and drift too close.

Spreading the food between them, he placed a wrapped burger in front of Lirikai and tucked into his own. Eating around a mouthful of food, he pointed at the condiments, "Sauces and seasonings."

She nodded, unwrapping her burger, glancing at how he was eating and took a tentative bite. "Much better than cafeteria offerings."

He chuckled at that, pulling some fries from another package.

He let her eat in peace, resisting interrogation mode, and observing instead. She was petite, with delicate features. If he hadn't seen it himself, he would never have believed anyone that had described the vicious teeth that erupted from her full lips earlier that evening. She looked like any number of women he'd met with surf boards in tow. Clearly a water baby, with the lean build to support the passion. He doubted she knew what a surf board was, never having needed one.

She sat back with a sigh.

"Tell me of yourself," Carson prompted.

When she looked at him, her expression turned wary, "There is nothing to tell. I live in the sea, I've been asleep."

His voice softened, "you said you had sisters—lost sisters."

Her finger poked at the condensation beading her cup. She nodded.

"Are they all," he hesitated, "dead? Are you the last?"

He watched her throat work before answering, "I don't know. I think so."

He considered this. "Are you a Mer-person?"

Her gaze met his, "No. I am Barra'kidai."

He blew a breath out as he sat back, a chill sweeping his spine.

Barra'kidai!

He'd heard the legends, but in all his centuries, he'd never met one.

Fierce and terrible, the Barra'kidai were the weapons of the sea Goddess' justice.

Carson's kind was created to protect. Lirikai and her kin were avengers.

Despite all the questions tumbling through his head, none would form as he stared at her, her expression burning into his memory. She was fierce, but he could see the underlying loneliness in her. The loneliness that drove her into hibernation. When he was still enough, he could feel it pull at him.

She dropped her face into her hands, took a deep breath pushing her hands through her hair and sat back with a long exhale. "Ask what you want to know."

"Could one of your sisters be responsible for the victims being left on the beach - the one we saw tonight?"

"Maybe. Yes," she relented, "but it is all wrong."

"How do you mean?"

"No one should ever know about this man's death. The Barra'kidai lure their intended to the sea. The ritual is never for the public..." she hesitated, her hands fluttering in front of her, searching for the right words. "It's as though something isn't right. The natural process has been disrupted or broken."

He waited for her to continue.

"We mete out Justice. We track a target, one who has done terrible deeds, and make them disappear from the world. They deserve no memory, only obliteration. Once we have them in the water, we rip them to shreds with our teeth and devour them until there is nothing left."

"Except their head."

She nodded. "The offering. In our human form, we return to the land, shave the hair from the back and carve the Goddess' mark, so that only she will know the identity of the prosecuted; that we have fulfilled our duty to her. The victims of the guilty will no longer live under their exploitation. It is their prayers to the Goddess that activate our mission. The completion of this part on land brings it full circle."

"The legend I'd heard was that you were all once human women?"

"Most of us were women. Not all. We were people of the seas, living along the coastal waters, honoring the Goddess. Pirates and raiders targeted our settlements. Some of us were her priestesses. Taken from our temples and villages and used violently and then left to the seas. She breathed her magic into some of us. In the sea, she gave us the form of the Barracuda, fierce and terrifying, devouring the dredges of humanity so that the innocent of heart may flourish and live peacefully."

She gave a short laugh. "For a long time, we descended with vengeance on those that had destroyed our lives. There was some balance established, but it didn't last. The exploiters of the world continued on; our work was never ending."

She took a sip of her drink. "And then there came a time where there just weren't enough of us to continue, and by then the Goddess had gone away." She stifled a yawn.

"So, the question is, why is the body on the beach?"

"Yes."

"What do you think the answer is?

"I'm not sure. But it is very concerning. As much as I want to go back to the ocean, I should find out what is happening."

THE SPY HID AMONG the rocky dunes watching. Waiting, breath shuddering, hands trembling.

The scene below was on display under the harsh spot lights. First the beach joggers, out for their evening ritual, discovering the remains. Cell phones extracted, emergency number dialed. Sirens and lights, and then investigators swarming the area. It hadn't taken long before the yellow tape went around a wide perimeter and the tent and white suits appeared to protect the exposed area from further contamination.

Isn't this what they were looking for? The signs, the brutality, the evidence.

Crouched behind rocks and tall tufts of grass, the spy searched among the personnel for a familiar face. A familiar scent. Anything that would lead them to the one that started it all.

Two individuals in casual civilian clothing parked above the scene, picked their way down, and merged with the crowd. The tall male had been to some of the more recent crime scenes. The small female was new.

Piqued, the spy's attention homed in on the tent where the newcomer disappeared, to reappear some minutes later, nearly tearing the white suit from her body. The tall male followed close, stopped, pulled her aside, brought her closer to where the spy lurked. Turned as they were, the excess light from the spot lights illuminated the woman's features. Their short conversation couldn't be heard over the surf. But her face. The spy's heart soared.

Not the expected face, no—this face, the spy had expected never to see again.

She was leaving with the tall man, heading back toward the jeep parked on the rise.

With a last glance over the scene, the spy made the quick decision to leave their intended observational position and break cover, running low behind the rocks and dunes for their own vehicle, making it just in time to see which way the jeep had gone. They followed at a safe distance, hands drumming the steering wheel, excited.

SEVEN

BEFORE THEY GOT BACK into Carson's vehicle, he made a quick call to leave a message for Ana. He hadn't expected her to pick up, but he briefed her on the scene and Lirikai's intention to work with them.

"Be careful Carson. She's volatile."

"Don't worry."

"And those teeth! Does nothing phase you? I think she could pierce even *your* hide, or do serious damage if you make the wrong move."

"Hey, you know me, I'm an island. I can handle whatever the sea throws at me."

"Funny."

He let his gaze wander to Lirikai belting herself into his car. "I can handle myself." He paused, "Hey, you're about the same height, aren't you? Do you think you'd have some clothes she could borrow for a few days?"

"Height, yeah. But she'd stretch my clothes out in places I enviably can't." He heard her sigh, then she relented, "I'll have a look. And before you ask, no she can't stay at my place. I live in a bachelor and Antony is here on leave. I'll see if the office will cover lodgings for her, but the new captain, he's pretty tight on the reins."

"Understood. Thanks, Ana."

"You owe me new clothes if she ruins mine." "Deal." He disconnected the call and dropped his phone into his pocket before sliding into the driver's seat. Once back on the road, he broached the subject of where she would stay. "Lirikai, I don't live around here. I'm contracted in to work on this case, then I get to go back home. But while I'm here, the locals put me up in a hotel."

She looked at him curiously.

"Like a traveler's hostel—a lodge."

She nodded.

"Humans are curious folk, and it would look odd if I were appearing from the sea every morning and disappearing every night. Might cause a stir."

She rolled her eyes at him. "I have noticed that we are no longer respected as we once were and now live hidden among them. That has become clear in my short time here."

He cleared his throat, feeling warmth creep up his neck, "You're welcome to share my hotel room for the time being. There is a sofa-bed I can sleep on." He cast her a glance. Her expression was curiously bemused. "Ana agreed to lend you some clothes," he nodded toward his t-shirt and shorts draping her lithe figure.

She looked down at herself, shrugged and said, "That is acceptable."

"I'll talk to the captain about adding you to the payroll too. You'll need money."

"Currency?"

He nodded.

"It would be easier if *I* was the one to come and go from the sea each day," she groaned.

"You'll be fine," he smiled at her.

THEY ARRIVED AT A large concrete building cut with evenly spaced rows of windows. "Well, here we are," he said with an unexcited sigh.

"Lacks elegance."

"That it does. Come on," he said, reaching to grab the file from the pocket behind his seat, then untie the surfboard from the back of the jeep. When he noticed her interested gaze on the board, he explained "It's a surfboard. People use them to float and ride the ocean waves standing up. It's fun," he insisted.

She smiled as she looked at him. They both knew how exhilarating it was to race the ocean, "Camouflage?"

He laughed, "Yes. But you should try it, it really is fun."

"Maybe."

They walked in through the lobby to the steel doors of the elevator banks. He drew the key card from his pocket and stepped in. After a moment's hesitation, she stepped in beside him, warily glancing around the interior of the confined space.

He remembered the first time he'd stepped into one, decades ago. He didn't care for the steel cages either. As soon as the doors opened again, she darted out.

"That was unpleasant."

"They're useful." He led her to a door toward the end of the long hall of identical doors, swiped the card and pushed the door open. She jumped when the heavy door slammed closed behind her. Her eyes were wide when he flicked the light switch on and gestured toward the large bed dominating the room. "You can sleep there."

Setting the surfboard out of the way, he dropped the file folder on the desk next to his laptop.

When he turned around, he saw her gaze considering the sofa.

"It opens into a bed," he moved forward to remove the cushions, and pulled the bed out. There was little space left in the small room.

After a moment, she looked up at him, "Thank you, Carson. I can sleep there, it is more than enough for me. You take your proper bed."

"I insist," he cleared his throat, turning the key card over between his fingers. "The lavatory is through that door if you wish to wash. Glancing at his watch, he said, "It's pretty late and I have to be back at the station early to go over the reports from tonight's scene."

Lirikai nodded and disappeared into the bathroom.

Carson dropped the car keys on the dresser and pulled a clean t-shirt and boxers from the top drawer. With a quick knock on the door, he reached his clothes in through the narrow opening.

"There's a spare hotel toothbrush still on the counter."

As soon as he pulled his hand back, the door shut.

With a sigh, he wandered to the desk, switched on the light and settled in to review the file he'd taken from his office and the emails on his laptop.

He heard the water running in the bathroom and did his best to block out the sound, and the random thoughts of Lirikai bathing that his imagination conjured. It was difficult, already having the image of her dripping wet in just a towel when he met her on the beach. All lithe limbs and silky skin.

He opened the file and began reviewing the case, which instantly scrubbed romantic images from his brain.

Opening his running word document on the case, he added notes about Lirikai, recording everything that had happened since he found her on the beach. He went over the events and information she'd given him, seeing how they fit into the case, trying to be as objective as possible.

He stared at the blinking cursor at the end of his last sentence. Objective. For all he really knew, *she* could be the one doing the killings. What did he *really* know of what she was? She could be spinning him a tale. He glanced at the bathroom door. The water was still running.

What had the Goddess of the Seas thrown at him this time?

He dropped his head with a groan, rubbing the back of his neck.

What was he getting himself into, here?

LIRIKAI NEARLY JUMPED OUT of her human skin, teeth erupting in self-defense, when a figure appeared from behind the lavatory door as she shut it.

It took a full moment for her senses to kick in enough to realize she was staring at her own image in the reflective glass set behind a counter. She stared at her Barra'kidai teeth projecting from her human face. How wonderfully monstrous she was! She jerked again at the rap on the lavatory door, followed by Carson's muffled voice. She opened the door just enough for his hand to appear bearing clothing. She snatched the fabric and snapped the door shut as soon as his hand disappeared.

Turning back to her own image, it dawned on her that she hadn't wanted Carson to see her as she was. Her appearance had never concerned her before, especially her Barra'kidai self. She was fiercely proud of the terror she instilled. This was what she was.

Did Carson find her teeth monstrous?

She turned away from the glass, instead assessing the white surfaces in the small room. It didn't take her long to figure out what they were for once she began twisting the silver knobs and levers. She surmised what the chair-like apparatus was for as she watched the water disappear then refill. Brilliant! From the large basin, the gush of water was a pleasant surprise and she was careful about the knobs that ejected pre-boiled water. The metallic overhanging flower imitated warm rain water. She dropped her borrowed clothing on the cold floor and stepped into it.

Some of these new experiences were worth awakening from the sea, at least for a little while. Gritty sand and bits of seaweed littered the basin by the time she turned off the water, and she wriggled her toes in it as it ran down into a small hole, then reached for a clean linen hanging from the wall, tucking it around herself.

Her thoughts returned to Carson, just beyond this small room. Just a few hours ago, she'd stepped out of the sea and into a completely new world. A world where she wasn't sure she belonged anymore. The Barra'kidai had ceased to serve their function before she went to sleep—it was the reason she'd gone into hibernation.

So, what now?

She'd somehow stumbled onto a beach where the Goddess-scented man had seemed to be waiting for her. Humans were being killed by someone that seemed to be a deranged Barra'kidai. Where was the Goddess pushing her toward? Her instinct told her she needed to see this through. Were it truly a Barra'kidai, only a Barra'kidai rightfully should handle it. If it were not, then who would besmirch the Barra'kidai in such as way? She wouldn't allow it to continue either way. It was her duty to discover what was happening and carry out justice. Perhaps the Goddess had pushed the ocean man into her path to awaken her to fulfill this duty.

She reached for the fresh clothes dropped on the counter. As she unfurled the new tunic, Carson's scent wafted under her nose. She brought it closer to her face. He smelled so good. He smelled like Goddess power, and...desire.

She jerked her feet into the other piece of clothing, hauling them up to cover her bottom. Catching her reflection again her eyes lingered on the plain fabric that was soft to the touch and smelled of him. These were his clothes. He wore them - over his naked flesh. She felt her cheeks tingle. As long as she'd been hibernating, it was even longer since she'd caressed a man. Retrieving the worn clothing from the floor, she didn't know what to do with them, so she folded and left them on the counter top. Opening the lavatory door, she headed straight for the bed Carson had indicated she should take, slid under the blanket, and turned toward the wall.

After a few moments, she heard Carson shuffle toward the lavatory and close the door.

When she heard the hiss of water, her imagination got creative.

She squeezed her eyes shut, determined to sleep.

EIGHT

AT SUNRISE, CARSON SHOWED Lirikai what to do with the toothbrush. They stood side by side in the bathroom, toothpaste foam rimming their mouths. Lirikai struggled not to gag on the stuff, as she stared at him awkwardly in the reflective glass. He smiled at her around the movement of his brush. He bent to spit, rinsed his mouth with water from the spout, "better?"

She copied his movements and nodded.

"Okay, lets grab a bite to eat, then get back to the station. You can change into some of Ana's clothes when we get there," he said, slipping straps over his shoulders to hold a pistol, and putting a leather folder into his pocket.

"That is acceptable," Lirikai mumbled, trying to scrub dribbled toothpaste from the front of Carson's borrowed t-shirt with a small cloth, leaving a wet patch.

He handed her a plastic key card, "you may need this if I'm not around. Keep it with you." He showed her how it opened the door.

She slipped her feet into the sandals Carson had loaned her the night before, and boarded his car. They collected food from a window in a brightly painted building and merged onto a road crammed with other cars like their own, moving slower than a sea slug.

Craning her neck to see over the cars ahead of them, she remarked, "Wouldn't it be faster to run there? It can't be so far?"

"It's a little farther than you would think. Be patient."

"Not my strongest characteristic."

"Clearly."

She narrowed her eyes at him, eliciting a deep chuckle. Giving up the scowl after a moment of appreciating the golden hue of his profile under the morning sun, she said, "tell me something of yourself."

He cast her a quick glance, apparently startled by the question. He made a lane change and passed several cars, and she thought he might not answer.

"Not much to tell. I lead a mostly mundane life among humans now, doing my duty to protect them when I can, but mostly from others like us—others that are more powerful than humans. Now, I mostly let humans protect themselves from other humans. I help where I can."

His shrug pulled at something in her. Humbleness.

"You know I am Barra'kidai. Who are your people?"

She watched the corner of his mouth and jaw tighten. His body lost its relaxed posture and he shifted himself more upright in his seat. The jeep accelerated, passing several more cars before darting back into slower traffic.

Lirikai turned her face away from Carson, watching the passing cars and greenery under the rising sun. Even at this hour, heat shimmered over the landscape.

"My people are the humans I watch over," he said after such a long time that the sound of his voice startled her from the reverie she'd drifted into.

She didn't press him.

On their return to the station, Lirikai was surprised to still see the main room full of criminals. There seemed to be an unending supply. As she followed Carson through the crowded space, her senses were as overloaded as they had been the night before. Mind you, not everyone in the room smelled tasty—not many at all, but some of them were overwhelming the room. By now, she observed who the 'cops' were and who Carson's 'perps' were, based on their demeanor and how some were dressed. The cops had pistols like Carson's. With others, the divisions weren't so clear. She felt drawn toward one or two so-called 'cops' that smelled more appealing than they should.

Was this the new world? To her instincts, it seemed that that deeply corrupt part of humanity hadn't abated over the centuries. It had merely adapted. As she passed among the men, some turned and smirked, giving her the up and down, others scowled, and yet others politely moved aside to let her pass with a 'Good morning'.

"Lirikai!" Ana's clear voice called to her over the din, cutting through the building haze of hunger.

She looked around, she didn't see Carson. Assuming he'd gone to his own small room, she headed toward Ana's door. It was a relief when the door closed on the noise.

"Here," Ana shoved a folded pile of fabric into Lirikai's hands. "These are the best hope I have of anything fitting your frame. There's more in that bag, and some shoes in the one on the floor."

"Thank you," Lirikai said in English, slipping the sandals from her feet while trying to peek through the clothes. "What is best for daytime?" she said gesturing at her the t-shirt and shorts she'd put on from the day before."

"Right, well, what you're wearing won't do, of course you know that. You'll want some work clothes, I suggest these, or these." Ana reached for the pile, separating and plopping the selections onto her neat desk. "There are undergarments in the other bag, although those I'm far less confident will fit you at all, but it was worth a try." She shrugged. "Oh! Oh, you're doing this right here, let me lock the door then." Ana bolted for the door, snapping the lock in place as Lirikai's t-shirt landed on one of the chairs in front of the desk, followed by the shorts.

Ana rushed across the windows, turning all the blinds before anyone noticed the naked woman in her office. She quickly retrieved the bag from the floor, ransacked the neatly folded underclothes and shoved a pair of panties in front of Lirikai, "like your shorts, but underneath."

Lirikai nodded in thanks and slipped into them.

Next, she pulled a bra free and Lirikai stared blankly at the thing, "That is clothes?" she said doubtful.

"Yes, uhm, here, I'll help you...?"

Again, Lirikai nodded, becoming rather bemused by Ana's awkward attempts to move around her without looking at or touching her.

Ana slid the thing over her arms, trying to position it properly without much success, "Uhm, those go in the cupped bits," she instructed waving her index finger at her exposed breasts. With Lirikai's help, Ana fastened the back.

"Why we need this?"

"Who knows," Ana muttered, "Customary to keep things in check."

They managed to get her into a skirt and blouse. Ana showed her how the top button worked, leaving her to the rest as she retrieved a couple pairs of shoes. "There are sneakers for walking and running in the bag, these are better for work."

Lirikai looked at the shoes, and stepped into the first pair, wobbled, tried the next, then abandoned both pairs for the sandals.

"Okay," Ana said with a nod. She stuffed the shoes back into the bag, then collected the rest of the clothing and put it in the other bag. "Well, everything almost fits," she tucked a lock of hair behind her ear, inspecting Lirikai. Now, with her model dressed, she freely tugged and shifted the fabric into place. "You definitely fill things out more than I do, so it may feel a little snug. The skirt is a bit shorter than appropriate, but I'm sure you'll be just fine." She bit her lip, looking Lirikai over. "Can you sit?"

Lirikai dropped into the cleared off chair, watching as Ana studied her with a frown, then pushed her knees together, encouraged her to sit straight, shoulders back, stomach in. "I go back to the sea," Lirikai huffed after several minutes. "These things are torture."

"No, you'll be fine. Honest." She fussed over Lirikai another minute, "Hair! May I?"

Lirikai looked at her dubiously, her eyes following her hand to a brush that had been placed on the desk. She nodded. She closed her eyes and relaxed after Ana's gentle touch moved the brush through her hair.

Tears stung her eyes and she sniffled a little. "I'm sorry! Did I pull too hard?"

"No, no, you're fine. I—I just haven't—No one but my sisters has ever brushed my hair for me."

Ana's voice softened, "Shall I let you do it yourself?"

"No, please continue, if you would."

She continued in silence, Ana's hands gently fluttering about Lirikai's head. She began to hum as she lifted and shaped Lirikai's hair into a style fit for the work place. "All finished," she said with a final pat.

"Thank you, Ana."

Ana's body language had shifted drastically in those last moments. She no longer fluttered, but moved with more ease, letting her small hand rest a moment on Lirikai's shoulder. She smiled, and Lirikai smiled back at her.

The door jerked against the lock, there was a knock, "Ana? Is Lirikai with you?"

"Hold on," she rushed over to let him in, then moved aside to reopen the blinds.

Carson stepped in, his gaze turning immediately to Lirikai. She stood. His eyes followed her. He swallowed hard, clearing his throat, shifting a sheaf of papers from one hand to the other.

"Doesn't she look great?"

"Much more appropriate than my T-shirt and shorts."

"Listen, I have some work I need to do off-site. I'll put these bags in your jeep when I head out, but before I go, Captain Mack wanted a meeting with you, and yesterday's site crew will send their report over as soon as they can."

"I've already got some of it." he held up the pages.

"Good, if there's anything else you need, you have my cell number." She let her gaze shift between Carson and Lirikai. She touched Lirikai's shoulder again and smiled, "I hope you don't return to the sea too soon." Ana picked up the bags and Carson closed the door behind her.

"Looks like you made a friend," he grinned.

Lirikai shrugged, "She is very likable."

He held up the folder, "Shall we?" He put it on the desk, and began flipping through the pages of solid text, passing a finger over some lines. "The first victim had a record, while the second didn't; he was a leader in his community. But this perp was known to the local police as an informant. Initially the other investigators thought these were random drug induced attacks, but now they're thinking it might be a little more organized."

Lirikai listened, not sure if this should mean anything to her.

Carson went on, "This escalation could mean more investigators working the cases from other departments who deal with gangs and drugs, potentially interfering with my work." He looked up from the file to Lirikai, "If one of your sisters is involved, this could get more difficult. I may lose my autonomy with these other departments around."

"I don't think they would figure out if she is involved, but what will happen to whomever they catch?"

"The killer will be taken into custody and go through a lengthy trial process and when found guilty, be imprisoned for the rest of their lives. If they catch someone and discover they aren't human, it would drastically change how they are treated. We need to avoid this at all costs." He stood and walked to the windows, looking into the inner bullpen where colleagues were processing perpetrators. "My job is to seek out individuals like us, and Ana helps me get them into the custody of our agency. No one else here knows about us—that we're not human—and we need to keep it that way."

"I miss the old days when we were respected, but I know in the last centuries, humans' fear has begun to push them to hunt and kill us. If my sister is involved, I will handle it. If it is someone else, then it is up to you."

"Lirikai, even if this is your sister's doing, I have to take her in to my agency. That's how it works."

She stared at him, anger tightening her chest muscles, "I don't work in your system."

"Everyone works in our system. It is the way the world works now." He frowned back at her.

"Not the Barra'kidai."

LIRIKAI'S BEST CHANCE TO find out if this was the work of one of her Barra'kidai sisters was by working with Carson and accessing the information he was being given.

A thrill shot down her spine. A sister!

The centuries had been so very long, especially with the absence of their Goddess. Lirikai thought herself to be the last of the Barra'kidai. She was among the first and had come to believe she was the last. If she had a sister walking the land, she needed to know. And if that sister was in need, she had to help her.

Her stomach dropped as she remembered the body on the beach. If this was her sister attacking these humans, there was something very wrong and she absolutely needed to find out what it was. If this wasn't her sister, then equally she needed to find out who was imitating a Barra'kidai.

She wasn't sure if she hoped it was a sister or not. Regardless, it wouldn't be an easy reunion.

No matter what the circumstances, something was very wrong. As she'd told Carson, the Barra'kidai didn't attack on land but far below the surface, away from any potential spectators, traces to be swept away. It meant whoever it was might not be able to fully shift into the sleek form of the Barracuda, with powerful jaws to rend and sever the guilty and deliver justice to the Goddess and her believers, those vulnerable humans that prayed to her for aid and vengeance when they could not achieve it for themselves. Or, *they* were the one being attacked and forced to defend themselves – to the death.

She had been one of those weak humans at one time. Despite the millennia, certain memories from her time as a human were seared into her consciousness. As a faithful priestess at the village temple, perched on an exposed cliff over-looking the seas, she was there daily making offerings and performing communal duties. Her husband tended the fields when he was not hunting, and together they took their turn tending the village children, providing respite for the elders who normally rounded them up and kept them in line.

A smile touched her lips, lost in her past. The crystal-clear memory of her husband before he was taken from her so long ago.

The raiding had begun. Again. They had enjoyed peace and free commerce for half a generation. The first whispers reached them when peddlers arrived for market day, bearing sad news of attacks along the coast in other places.

The elders immediately called on the village council to confer. They knew what was coming, they'd seen it before. The younger, like herself, had their childhood memories of the last attack, and while nervous, most didn't believe they'd really return to this village. They had no riches, there was nothing here of value for them. Their temple was modest and precious items were no longer prized offerings to the

Goddess at this location. Instead, the priestesses devoted their time, heart and faith to her, and life had been good. Until now.

There was some resistance to extreme action, but in the end, it was decided that militia duty would double. Able bodied adults would assemble for practice as soon as they were finished their work in the fields. Those that could not fight would begin work on defenses.

But it was too late. Before anything could properly begin, the attack came in the night. The priestesses had also added to their temple duties by staying at the cliff top in long hours of prayers and offerings, pleading to the Goddess to save them from those that would harm them.

While assembled in meditation and prayer, the attack had come. The black sails were invisible on the dark waters. The natural crashing of surf and wind swallowed shouts and the clashing of weapons.

As soon as one of the priestesses realized what was happening, they grabbed their spears, running from the temple down the long winding path to the village. It was too late, the roofs of the mud-brick houses were ablaze, bodies strewn wherever they fell. Most held weapons of some kind in an attempt to defend themselves, but not all. Nearly all the elderly had been slain, and anyone that wasn't hale and whole of body lay dead and dying among them. The youngest of the children, unable to care for themselves, were littered among the elders who'd tried to save them.

Lirikai's infant niece lay in a pool of her aged father's blood, who'd died trying to protect his granddaughter. Her mind in a haze of grief and rage, she sought out her husband and young brothers, who had also been slain while protecting the village.

The priestesses rallied on the beach, fury and grief in their faces as the raiders corralled their booty to take on board their ships. There were no resources of trade value to be found in this village. Its people were its most valued commodity, and it seemed that was what the attackers had been seeking. Healthy, strong stock to trade into servitude, chained together, being pushed into the boats.

On seeing the priestesses gathered with their spears, they laughed and turned to engage them. They fought as hard as the militia had, to no avail. They too were captured and chained.

Aboard the ships, they were crowded into spaces meant for inanimate cargo, not people, and the sails turned them away from their burning village. By the time the shore line was lost in the haze of ocean mist mixed with smoke, the attackers turned their full attention on their goods.

They sought to defile and break the priestesses to gain their submission and that of their surviving villagers.

Every one of the Priestesses were terribly used and slain, their bodies dumped into the ocean.

Lirikai remembered every moment.

She remembered her death.

The seconds before her heart ceased to beat, she stood outside herself, still attached to the emotions, still feeling the agonizing pain throughout her body. One by one, beside her appeared her sisters outside their corporeal forms, watching as their white limbed bodies sank below the surface of the water, the cries of the grief-stricken villagers wailing around them. They had tried to defend what was left of their village, to save those that would be used and violated by these horrible raiders.

In the end, the villagers were not broken into submission, but called to the Goddess to vindicate their injustice in memory of their faithful priestesses. They made a last effort to attack their captors, fighting to their deaths.

Lirikai's next memory was of standing on the ocean floor before a formless being of energy which swirled before her and her slain sister-priestesses, their bodies drifting in the water above them.

Thought intruded into their minds collectively. This swirling mass of energy before them was their Goddess. The thoughts were overwhelming initially, emotions of tired fury rippled through the water. The Goddess' energy wavered and shifted from form to form—elegant blue scales and fins to graceful human limbs and hair, then back again.

Now when Lirikai recalled, as ancient and overwhelming as the Goddess felt even then, she now recognized the signs of a being that was beginning to fade.

She had made us before drifting away, even then.

Their bodies, floating above their ethereal heads, jerked in the current, and directed by the change in energy, gathered in a swirling collection, their pale lifeless selves were flashes of light in the darkness of the ocean floor in the darkest of the night.

"You shall be feared. You shall be the seekers of justice in this unjust world. Each individual has the gift of free will, and to abuse such a thing to violate another is an aberration."

Lirikai watched in fascination as the corpses twisted in the seawater, hair and limbs melding to their bodies, reforming into sleek silvered scales with razor sharp fins. She recognized the form of the barracuda; a creature feared among the villagers for its fierce teeth and its vicious and calculated attacks on its prey. The strong jaws and terrifying teeth able to sever limbs and snap bones.

She stared at the beautifully terrifying new form her body had become.

The goddess gave them their instruction. They may change into their human forms to complete their missions: To capture those that would exploit the innocent, drag them into the ocean and devour them until there was nothing left of their existence. Without a body to litter the land, humanity would forget those deemed unworthy to be remembered. Instead let the victims be the focus of memory. The guilty to fade and be forgotten. Their heads to be marked and remitted to the Goddess so that she may pass judgment on their souls.

Their new bodies ceased twisting in the currents above them, and their spirits were slammed back into them. Oh, the bliss of swimming as the newly formed Barra'kidai. The powerful sleek bodies. The power in their jaws.

Collectively, they twisted their bodies, and swam straight for the boats, following, plotting, luring, until every one of the attackers disappeared below the ocean surface, their heads piled at the Goddess' deep-sea cave.

These priestesses had fought and died together for their Goddess and for their families and village. Reborn, they only had each other, and remained so for centuries. In the early decades, the Goddess would periodically find another to add to their group. Some of them were lost in battles, doing their duty. They fought to the death every time.

They secured their coast, and with legends of terrifying monsters in the waters of their home areas, raiding eventually stopped. Their original village had been destroyed, but their neighbors had come to bury the dead and perform the rites. Some of the nearby villages had daughters and sons who'd been born in Lirikai's village, and some returned to begin anew.

All this time later, she wondered if it still existed.

She'd not been back since long before she'd lost her sisters.

The last couple had reclaimed their humanity. They'd told her, that they had felt a shift in their hearts that they had finally achieved true justice for themselves. She couldn't fathom what that meant. She didn't believe she could ever feel that she would achieve justice for her husband, her aged father, her niece and siblings. She would never have justice for what was done to her village. It was too much. Her family could never be replaced in her heart. She had loved them with everything that she was. There was no heart left to offer to a human life. There was only the Goddess and her sisters now. How could justice be complete without the return of life? She had been given another life—without her family. This second life had a purpose and she meant to fulfill it. She would honor what had been gifted to her. She would fight to the death every time.

If she truly still had a sister left, then it was her duty to help her.

Even if, as she feared, that sister was locked in a state trapped between human and Barra'kidai, unable to control the instinct, overriding a body unable to fully shift to fulfill that instinct.

If Carson had the means to track her sister in this confusing modern world, then she would work with him.

Lirikai would never turn her back on a Barra'kidai, especially a sister that needed her.

NINE

CARSON DIDN'T TELL LIRIKAI that the legends of the Barra'kidai had faded. That only he remembered them because he himself was so old. Lirikai was the last of her kind, except of course the possible killer. From what he suspected, if this was indeed the work of a sister, something was very wrong in terms of ritual.

Aside from the fact that dead humans were turning up mutilated.

Now he stood before the station captain, Bruce Mack. "You wanted to see me, sir?" Carson struggled to control his breathing. The room was heavy with the scent of the man's aftershave. It smelled like a teenage boy had gotten hold of the bottle.

The stocky man looked up from his desk, a perma-frown carved into his brow. "Sit."

Carson ignored his bark and took the chair, easing himself back, propping an ankle over his knee. He let out a steady breath, forcing himself to relax, wishing he'd left the door open.

He stared back at the captain, waiting for him to state the reason for his summons. Despite what seemed to be the man's naturally furrowed brow, the rest of him was unreadable. "I understand you've brought someone into the department to work with you, a woman? I wasn't briefed on her presence."

"Yes. I will be responsible for her."

There was a quick knock and the door opened. Mack frowned at the intruder.

"Another missing person report, sir."

"Give it to Keenan, she's working those cases," he waved the person out and returned his scowl to Carson.

"You've done good work for us before, so I'll forgive this oversight. In the future, I want to know before-hand who is coming unvetted into my precinct." The eyes staring at Carson were inscrutable, but the overpowering scent of aftershave was distracting.

Carson frowned; as GPSA agents, they worked with whomever they wanted. As far as the Captain knew, Carson was a federal agent.

Ana was the west coast staff liaison and she usually dealt with the captain. Carson hated office politics. His thumb started tapping is knee. He just wanted to do the job. Ana handled the egos. She was good at it.

"Yes sir," he said, dropping his foot to the floor, sitting forward. "Anything else?"

"Any suspects yet? You need any help, see officer Keenan. She's my right hand 'round here."

"Not yet, but we're working on it."

The older man gave a sharp nod and waved his hand.

Carson gladly accepted the dismissal, taking a deep cleansing breath as soon as he had the office door open.

They spent hours reviewing the photos, reports and accompanying documents for each victim.

He had the sense that key information was missing. The witness and family interviews were sparse, and the background checks bordered on vague.

A shady pawnbroker with a rap sheet, a minister, and a known police informant. What was their connection?

Carson stood, scrubbed a hand over his face, stretched, yawned and looked at his watch. "Call it a day?"

"What day?" Lirikai asked absently as she leaned over the desk studying the victim photos lined up side by side, trying to determine and confirm the bite pattern.

He smiled, "End of the work day. Are you hungry?"

"Famished, just fetch someone from the next room for me." She looked up, a twinkle in her eye.

He glanced out his office door. *For her it must be like walking through a kitchen with several ovens roasting a feast.* That was the best way he could think of it to understand. He imagined himself the last time he'd been through a kitchen with a roast chicken, or turkey, or beef and the mouth-watering scents surrounding him. Is that what Lirikai experienced? He eyed a couple of the scruffy looking guys from his vantage point and shuddered. Definitely not to his taste, but hey, who was he to judge?

He turned back to her and admired her form leaning over the desk in thought. Especially for someone who looked like she did.

She had looked hot in his shorts and t-shirt. Now she was a wild woman confined to form-fitting formal work clothing—so much hotter. His eyes lingered on the curve of her breast and hips where the fabric strained, and the elegant lines of her toned legs. He curled his hands, resisting the urge to slide his fingers up the smooth skin of her thigh, or splay his hands round her hips and narrow waist. He wondered what the sensitive flesh just behind her knee would taste like. He closed his eyes, breaking the thoughts.

Opening his eyes, he smiled as his gaze landed on his flip flops which were far too large for her feet.

"Is something wrong with my feet?"

His eyes shot back up to her face, "No, not at all. Shall we go now?"

"Yes." She turned to gather together the papers and photos, sliding them into folders.

As they made their way to the parking lot, Carson watched which way Lirikai's head turned as she scented. He recognized that she usually picked up on the worst felons, not the petty thieves or drunken rabble, whom she ignored all together, but the worst of the worst.

The ones intent on hurting others, or those willing to hurt others to get what they wanted.

He took the folders from her and tucked them into the usual pocket behind his seat while she went around to get into the jeep. Jumping in behind the wheel, he turned to check that she was in while he pulled his seat belt on, only to find that she was struggling to lift her leg, due to the unforgiving hem of the skirt. He was about to get out to help lift her in, when she yanked the skirt up, exposing the frill of her panties, and jumped in.

"Not practical," she murmured, trying to wriggle the fabric back down over her thighs.

Carson quickly turned his gaze away, swallowing hard, but the image of that little bit of lace on her silky skin was seared into his mind. His fists gripped the steering wheel as he struggled to focus. Where were they going? Right, food! But all he could think about was putting his mouth on that silky flesh where it met the lace trim.

"Carson?" Her voice was a question of concern. "Are you unwell? Your skin has gone pink."

He tossed her a smile, "I'm good, no worries. Where shall we go?"

She shrugged, "Since I have no money, I can always go to the sea and eat some fish."

"I recall I promised you a steak," relieved for that flash of memory, he latched on to it.

She nodded, "That is acceptable."

As he started the car and put it into gear, she reached into the back seat for the bags of clothing Ana had stowed there for her. "I wonder if there is something more comfortable," she said, rummaging through it. They hit a pothole, and she struggled to keep the clothing from being tossed around the jeep.

"Maybe look later when we have light and space." He said, upon seeing bras and panties spilling onto Lirikai's lap.

She huffed and stuffed everything back into the bag, tossing it into the backseat.

Moments later, they pulled into the parking lot of his favorite steak joint, overlooking the ocean. In an instant, he was around to Lirikai's door, opening and lifting her down out of the jeep. He smiled into her wide eyes as she gripped his shoulders in surprise. "Thought I'd save you the struggle."

She had flecks of silver and green in her eyes and tiny freckles across the bridge of her nose. She swayed, catching her balance as he set her on her feet, sending the heat and scent of her to encircle him. His nostrils flared as he inhaled, staring at her lips.

His hands flexed open, releasing her, and he stepped back.

Closing the jeep door, her gaze on his face was intent.

He gave her an awkward smile, "This way." He motioned toward the front door of the restaurant.

Inside, they were settled at a small table set into a window alcove for privacy. Carson explained what was on the menu.

"This is all new, I will try what you recommend."

He asked her several more questions about her preferences, gave the waiter their order, and asked for a bottle of wine.

"Wine!" she exclaimed, rubbing her hands together, "I recall I enjoy it."

He admired her broad smile, pleased that he had found something she liked. He struggled to find some topic to chat about other than the case. Most general modern cultural references or subjects would be meaningless to her. He wanted to keep the conversation light. "Tell me of where you've been."

"Everywhere warm."

"Favorite place?"

She thought a moment, a small frown marring her smooth forehead. "My home village."

The waiter returned with glasses of water, then brought glasses for their wine and opened the bottle, pouring the first glass for them. When he left, she told Carson of several places that she had been to that were beautiful. He'd been to a few of them himself.

"Have you ever traveled inland?"

She shook her head. "Always ocean and coastal lands."

By the time the steak arrived, their conversation had progressed, and Carson was enjoying learning more about some of the places she'd been to that he hadn't, and with those that he had, they compared experiences through their first glasses of wine.

"This is wonderful," Lirikai gushed, her mouth full of steak. "So much better than raw fish."

He winked at her, saluting her with his beef-laden fork as he chewed.

She asked him about his work, and he told her about some of his more interesting cases and colleagues with the Global Paranormal Security Agency.

Their plates cleared, wine bottle empty, they appeared to be having a wonderful evening, like any of the other companions in the dining space.

"It has been so long since I've had wine, I am not sure I can stand up now," Lirikai giggled.

"Let me help you, Lirikai" Carson stood, his hip bumped the table with less grace than he intended, drawing a giggle from Lirikai.

"Liri, my friends called me Liri."

He smiled, "Liri, then."

Outside, the ocean air immediately encircled them, enticing and fresh. Liri stood eyes closed inhaling deeply. "I will never tire of that smell."

"Shall we go down for a walk?"

Her face lit up and she immediately set off toward the path winding down to the beach. The wine and good food relaxed his body, allowing him to enjoy the evening more thoroughly. The case and his responsibilities were a foggy memory, better left for tomorrow. Tonight, he was going to enjoy a few leisurely hours in the company of this fascinating and beautiful woman.

Following her down the path, he smiled when she turned back to see if he was close behind, her own face aglow with moonlight, a satisfied belly, and a little too much wine. As soon as he was close enough, she grabbed his hand and pulled him toward the water. Once the ocean lapped at her feet, she stopped and turned toward him. Her face was so open he could see how at ease she was, too.

"I have not felt this wonderful in such a long time—I had forgotten it was possible."

"Me too." He smiled down into her face.

He was taken off guard when she grabbed his face, pulled him to her and kissed him, and just as quickly, before his arms could trap her, she released him again. "Thank you."

His chest tightened considering her joy, his groin tightened from the sensation of her mouth on his and the invasion of her scent burning into his memory.

"What?" Her words had come to him in a haze of confused happiness and desire.

"I said we should swim." She was already reaching for the buttons of her shirt.

"Wait," he managed before she could divest herself. "We can't let anyone see us."

"Oh, yes," she immediately turned, seeking some area of seclusion. In the distance there was a rocky outcrop. She laughed and started

running, the flip flops kicking up sand behind
her.

Pulling his shoes and socks off, he ran after
her. She skidded to a halt and scrambled over
the rocks. His heart was pounding in his ears
when he caught up to her. The outcrop formed
a small shielded 'U' open to the ocean. She was
already down to her undergarments and he
stood transfixed a moment. Shaking himself,
he turned away and set his shoes into a safe
place in the rocks, then pulled his pants off,
ensuring his keys and wallet were safely tucked
into the pockets and hoped someone didn't discover and take off with them. Next his shirt, and
with a glance on seeing she was divested of her
bra and panties, he tugged his shorts off and
stuffed them in the rocks with her bundle of
clothes.

She was gone in the space of time it required
to secure the clothes. With a shrug, he set off for
the water. He almost didn't care if there were
others around. He too hadn't felt this free in a
long time. Even when he shifted and swam the
deepest parts of the ocean to rid himself of his
worries, he wasn't so befuddled and clear all at
once.

There was something about the last hours together that he felt had caused something in himself to shift. And she seemed to have been affected by it too.

A sense of abandon.

Maybe it was the wine.

Maybe it was Liri.

He moved into the water and she surfaced, drawing breath. Being in the ocean, he could feel the Goddess energy shimmering in her, calling to his own. It radiated between them.

He swam out to where she treaded water, her face pale against the darkness of the sea and sky.

"Do you know what I haven't done in a long time?"

He shook his head.

"Raced. I want to race!" She laughed.

He couldn't stop the grin spreading across his face if he'd wanted to. "We should move to deeper water." He turned to quickly scan the beach, ensuring there was no one around that might mistake them for drunken swimmers about to drown themselves. Drunken maybe, but as to the risk of drowning; there was none as long as they shifted. He couldn't see anyone.

Lirikai had already dropped below the surface. He drew in a deep breath and dove, swimming farther out from the beach toward where the land shelf dropped away. Silver flashed in the darkness. He shifted.

TEN

LIRIKAI ENJOYED THE PLEASANT buzz from the wine and the satisfaction of a full belly. As Carson had promised, the steak was delicious. It certainly stayed the annoying hunger that had been gnawing at her since entering the precinct.

As Carson checked for potential witnesses, she let herself sink below the surface. Floating, she closed her eyes and let the Barra'kidai take over her form, excited by the prospect of a race. Her scales caught the diffused moonlight as she circled, waiting for Carson to slip beneath the surface.

She observed his muscled human form as he dove and swam out to meet her. She admired the power of his limbs as he swam, then was entranced as she watched his shift. The area around him shimmered, blurring the lines of his body. Goddess energy surged and permeated the water. It was much like watching her sisters take their Barra'kidai form.

A thrill shuddered through her body as he emerged. He was magnificent! He must have been at least ten times her size, with pearlescent scales, spikes along his back and tail, webbed feet tipped with claws that would frighten the fiercest of polar bears. His head was broad and fierce with dangerous teeth and a powerful jaw.

She felt dwarfed in his presence and she knew she wasn't a small creature.

A wave of self-consciousness thrummed through her. Would he find her ugly? She knew he was interested in her human form, but her Barra'kidai was vastly different.

He drifted in front of her. The sensation of the Goddess enveloping them, causing her fins and tail to tingle, reminding her she had challenged him to a race.

She darted up over his head and arched down, sliding her belly along the side of his neck ensuring she had his attention. Given his size, he could easily out pace her. She gave him a little flick of her tail against his neck as she drew away and burst forward leaving him in a cloud of ocean algae.

The ocean rumbled and he was upon her. She darted again relying on the power of her body and slick scales to out distance him, determined to stay ahead of him. The thrill of the race pushed her on. They had no end point. She could choose the heading and see how far he would follow or take the lead. This motivated her to swim harder. But where to?

Thoughts of her cave invaded her mind. She sought ocean bed features to orient herself and corrected her direction. Seconds later he was with her again. She let herself twist and tumble, slicing through the sea water toward her goal, ever deeper until the surface was just a passing thought.

She slowed when the familiar darkened shape appeared. Carson curled around her, clearly curious by the direction she'd gone. Floating into the mouth of the cave, she looked around it. Had it been a full day since she'd awakened and left this place? Already, despite all the decades she'd slumbered here, it was now the place that felt distant. It wasn't a large cave, just large enough for Carson to enter and curl up in the blackness. In here, the vibration of the energy between them intensified as it reverberated off the rock walls, permeating every cell in her body.

Could he feel it too?

The space, which for centuries had been a comfortable haven to her, suddenly felt far too small.

She darted back out of the cave mouth. Carson emerged, his eyes on her. She had the impression he was concerned.

Mischievousness returned in a rush and she darted forward, letting the tip of her tail fin slap his snout and she was off again. She swam hard, not looking back. Any time she started to lag, she pushed harder to out-pace him in any direction she shifted toward. If she'd been in her human form, she'd have been laughing like a carefree child.

Eventually, growing weary, she rose toward the surface and banked toward the rising ocean floor that would bring them back to the shoreline.

Once within a reasonable distance of shore, she shifted, then broke the surface to look around. Carson's head appeared beside her.

"Where are we?"

Lirikai laughed, "I haven't any idea!"

They floated next to each other, treading water, Carson surveyed the landscape. "I can't tell, have to get closer."

They swam in, angling toward an area where the land rose up. The moon was much lower in the sky and the beach appeared to be deserted.

He laughed then, "Damn, I think we swam too far."

"No matter." Lirikai tossed over her shoulder as she headed toward the beach. "We can just swim back again."

"Lirikai, we have no clothes, we can't go up on the beach in the nude."

"So modest. I just want to get close enough to touch bottom."

They stood facing one another, sand drifting over their feet, the ocean swaying them gently. Carson stepped forward. "That cave, was that where you were before? Before we met on the beach?"

She nodded, looking up into his face, sharp angles and smooth planes under the moonlight. She could still feel the energy of the goddess between them, making her skin tingle.

He took another step closer to her, causing all her skin to turn to goosebumps.

His eyes were dark as he regarded her, she felt his fingers trail up her arm beneath the water, up over her shoulder to her jaw. "Seemed like a lonely little place."

She shrugged, "It was quiet and dark. What I wanted."

"Do you still want that? Quiet darkness? Solitude?" his thumb stroked over her cheek.

Her breath hitched. How long had it been since anyone, let alone a man, touched her with tenderness?

"Not at the moment." She tilted her head back to see his face more fully.

His eyes swept her face, lingering on her lips. He was closer now. Her tongue slipped over her lips, wanting to taste his.

Fingers reaching, they tentatively danced over his bare chest. His next step brought him so close his body warmed the sea water between them.

Lirikai closed the gap between them. His lips met hers as her body pressed to his. Her mind was divided between the press of his lips, and the thrill of his body against hers, chest to chest, hip to hip, his arousal caught between them.

Desire shot through her body. She slid the tip of her tongue over his bottom lip, then met his.

He didn't hesitate once the invitation was made. His arms closed around her, his tongue and lips dominating her mouth.

The constant movement of the ocean kept their bodies sliding against one another. Her tight nipples grazed the taut muscles of his abdomen. Her hands trailed around the sensitive flesh of his ribs to slide over and up to his shoulder blades, then back down to his lower back and backside, eliciting a growl from deep in his chest. His hands were immediately on her hips, then her own backside, crushing her hard against him. His arousal pulsed between them, triggering her core to throb in response.

She wanted to climb him. Shifting so that her foot trailed up his calf, he grabbed her thigh, lifting it up to his hip. He stopped, looking down into her face, lips parted. The hunger in it matched her own. Her palms slid over his nipples as her hands found their way to his shoulders and neck, leaning into him. The ocean made her almost weightless as she locked her ankles behind him, her thighs gripping his hips, his member still between them, rubbing against her. His hands supported her bottom as he kissed her, working his way from her lips, along her jaw, down her throat and chest. Leaning back, she made room for his mouth to claim her breast, his tongue and teeth grazing over one taut nipple and then the other.

Reaching down between them, her hand gripped his shaft, making him growl again as she worked him. He sucked a little harder on her nipples and her grip on his shaft matched him. Until she could stand it no more and guided his tip to her entrance, trying to control her breathing.

Releasing her breasts, he looked up into her face as the grip of his hands on her bottom shifted to guide her down onto his shaft, filling her. They both groaned as they stared at each other, eye to eye.

This close to him, the moonlight illuminating his face, she could see something in his eyes that instinctively connected to that part of herself that knew what true solitude was, and that tentative desire to fill a longing which loneliness craved.

Since she'd been lured out of her lonely cave by the goddess energy, she'd reawakened to the shock of an alien world, been denied the temptation of her instincts, discovered she may yet still have a sister in a desperate state, and all of it was tied to this gorgeous man, who likely was the only one who had any sense of what she was in this world and what it meant. Her world had changed, and she no longer had a purpose in it. He was like her, and he was fully integrated into this world and had a role. Perhaps she could learn too. His strong hands supported her bottom as she leaned into him, her arms over his shoulders. One hand drifted to up his jaw and cheek as she looked into his eyes, her body slowly riding him.

She could see the hunger and tenderness as he looked into her face. She'd been with other men over the centuries, of course. A means to appease the body. Her primary companionship had been her sisters.

Carson elicited both possibilities. Would she eventually return to the cave? She kissed him, letting her tongue sweep his, moving faster, closing her eyes to blot out the thoughts and focus only on the feel of his body, the scent of him and the essence of his energy. She rode him, abandoning her concerns. She could sense the tension building in him and rode harder and faster. She could sense how close he was, the control he maintained over himself still. Her teeth grazed his shoulder, tongue tasting his flesh. She gripped him hard as her body exploded, rocking into him, denying herself the urge to claim.

As soon as her climax receded, Carson gripped her hips, thrusting into her swollen body, building to release. The second before he gave into orgasm, he claimed her mouth, withdrew from her body and gave his seed to the ocean. She kissed him thoroughly, but she felt a deep sense of loss at his sudden withdrawal. Once their bodies calmed, she unlinked her ankles and slid back to her feet.

Carson sighed, glancing at the angle of the moon. "It's late."

Her hands lingered on his shoulders and chest a moment longer. Stepping away from him, she turned and began to swim back to deeper water, Carson close by. She shifted, then felt the ripple of power envelope her as Carson shifted, causing her scales and fins to tingle.

As they swam back to the rocky alcove where they'd left their clothes, Carson's thoughts were completely absorbed with Lirikai. Her barracuda form was lithe and powerful and impressively fierce. He had no doubt how she and her sisters had instilled terror in the guilty as they doled out the Goddess' judgment.

Their love making had been so unexpected, yet in the aftermath of the wine and the heady race through the ocean landscape, it felt right. As soon as she'd stepped into his embrace, it all felt right. She was incredible. So solid in her identity and purpose. She knew who she was and what she was meant to do.

What would happen if they did find one of her sisters was responsible for the murders? He was certain it wouldn't go well. The Barra'kidai sisterhood was legendary. She would fight for her sister, and it was his responsibility to bring killers to justice. Could he make Lirikai understand how things worked now? He doubted he could. She hadn't been part of the new world long enough.

He glanced at her silvered eyes and sharp teeth. He would have to convince her. Somehow. Could he lock a Barra'kidai in a human prison?

Could he put her in a prison with murdering, exploitive convicts? It would drive her to the madness. Is this what was happening to the killer? Was it another Barra'kidai after all? Given what he'd seen of Lirikai, and what little he knew of their legend, he tried to imagine what would happen to her if she were put into a position where her instincts to deliver justice were overwhelmed, but she was incapable of completing her purpose. Would it look something like what they were encountering?

He suddenly understood they were indeed tracking another Barra'kidai. He had to bring her in to the GPSA.

The landscape of the ocean floor became familiar. They shifted back to human form and surfaced, swimming to the rocks they'd launched their race from. Her human form was as lithe and powerful as her barracuda. She walked through the surf with a languid grace. Admiring her naked form in the moonlight, his body reacted. When she bent to retrieve the clothes from the nook, he'd stuffed them into, his shaft bucked. They were still secluded, but looking at the rocks and sand, he doubted either of them would appreciate the grit on exposed flesh. She turned, clothes in hand, and mischief curled her lips as she glanced at his groin, shoving his clothes into his chest. She dressed, careful to leave the sand on the beach, taking longer than necessary. He gritted his teeth, realizing she was doing it deliberately, then chuckled, stepping forward to help fasten her bra. He kissed her bare shoulder then pulled the blouse from her hand. Slipping her arms into the sleeves, he turned her so he could fasten the buttons. She watched his face closely as he admired her breasts. Thankfully he managed to ensure the buttons were all aligned properly.

He gestured toward the rise where the restaurant and parking lot were. "Shall we?" His voice was tight.

Her smile was blinding when she turned to scramble back over the rocks to the smoother sand of the beach. His jeep was the solitary vehicle in the lot next to the restaurant, now locked up for the night. Openly admiring her figure in the office clothes Ana had given her, he was lost in the sway of her hips when she reached for the jeep door. An instant later, his hands were on her hips as he lifted her to the seat—to spare the skirt, he told himself, knowing it was really to touch her again. She grinned up at him, slid a hand up his arm and squeezed his bicep, her hand lingering with appreciation.

Already leaning into the enclosed cab, inches from her mouth with his face close to hers, he closed the distance. Her tongue slipped over her lip, tagging his. His free hand moved to her face. It was as though now that he'd touched her, he needed to touch her more. His body agreed. Hands itching to roam over her, he withdrew with a soft peck on her lips and a sigh. He closed the door and rounded the jeep to his own side.

The drive back was peaceful and silent. The only sounds were the engine and the wind and night creatures overlaying the constant surge of the ocean along the length of the coastal highway.

Back at the hotel, with Ana's bags of clothing in hand, through the lobby and elevator ride Lirikai said little to nothing. Carson began to worry that she was having second thoughts about their evening. His gut dropped. And if she did? Then he would let her go. It wasn't a contract. But he couldn't deny, he didn't like the idea of parting.

He glanced at her again. What was he thinking? She'd only walked out of the sea the day before, she'd been a potential suspect, quickly turned investigative partner with her own agenda, and they'd ended the day with dinner and sex.

Through the door, she went into the wash-
room, turning on the tub faucet. Dropping his
keys on the dresser, he scrubbed a hand over his
face. When had he become so impulsive and
careless? Probably right about the time Lirikai
appeared on the beach in nothing but a stolen
towel.

The water tumbled into the tub, then was cut
by the sound as it shifted to the shower head.
Lirikai emerged from the bathroom divested
of the blouse and skirt. His eyes roamed all over
the lace bra and panties as she leaned over the
bag of clothes on the end of the bed. Dump-
ing the bag, she rummaged through the fabric.
"Which one is for sleeping?"

Helping her shuffle through the clothes, he
cursed Ana's name under his breath. The clos-
est thing to pajamas he could find in the pile
was a very transparent negligee that dangled
from his forefinger. "I have more t-shirts if you
prefer."

She looked at the fabric dubiously, plucked
it from his fingers held it up to her chest casting him a sidelong glance. "Decide later." The
lingerie landed atop the pile as Lirikai grabbed
Carson's hand, pulling him into the bathroom
with her.

Well this is happening, again, already.

She was pulling his clothes from him, stitches tearing now and then. Propping her up on the counter, her breasts sprung free when he slipped the hooks of her bra, his mouth was quick to claim first one nipple then the other. He inhaled deeply the scent of ocean and their lovemaking that still clung to her skin, working his way down her tight stomach to the edge of her panties kissing her hip and the flesh along the edge of the lace. Pulling her off the counter, his fingers hooked the edges of the panties, pulling them down her legs so she could step out of them. His face drifted back up her legs and thighs, planting kisses along the way. She smelled so good, he couldn't resist. She gasped at the contact of his tongue, leaning back against the counter. Nudging her knees wider, his mouth fastened on her nub after a few tentative licks. Everything about her invaded his senses, the urge to devour her was strong.

By the time he was done with her, she was pliant in his care as he drew her toward the still running water of the shower, helping her step in. Picking up the soap, he lathered and bathed her flushed skin, then helped her wash the sea from her hair. As soon as she was clean, she took up the soap and returned the favor, carefully soaping every inch of him, paying special care to his perpetually erect shaft. It bucked with her every touch, when she knelt before him, he thought he was about to die. Her beautiful face was flushed with satisfaction, her lips, swollen from their kisses, opened and took him in. His hands shot out to brace himself against the shower walls as desire ripped through him hard and fast. It took everything he had to hold it back, reveling in her attentions. When he drew close, she licked his length, then worked her way up his abdomen and chest, claiming his mouth.

Then she turned around, braced her hands on the opposite wall and pushed her beautifully rounded bottom against his groin. His chest was tight. Slipping his fingers along the edge of her bottom he let them slide along her core, feeling how ready she was for him. He gave her hip a little squeeze, but instead of taking her against the shower wall, he turned off the water, and helped her out of the tub. Reaching for a towel, he wrapped it around her, ignoring the frown and confusion marring her lovely face. He kissed her nose and swept her up into his arms, putting her down on the bed, pushing the pile of clothing to the floor. He left her a moment to retrieve the condom from his wallet, letting it drop to the dresser top next to his keys.

Curiosity lit her face, her eyes on the package in his hands.

"Protection," he said, letting the wrapper drop to the bedside table as he quickly rolled the condom over his erection. "From what?"

"Children," he said, crawling up over her body.

"You don't need that."

He froze, his sheathed member hanging between them.

"I can't make children," she said.

He saw some emotion flutter across her face, but it was gone so quickly, he wasn't so sure. "That's alright, it's on now," he leaned in to kiss her as deeply as he could until her hands roamed and gripped and pulled at him.

"Carson," she whispered, her legs sliding up over his hips, her hands gripping his buttocks.

His tip at her entrance, he slid home and went still, his arms iron taut on either side of her as she groaned, her head rolled, lips parted. In effort to control his body, his tongue licked her parted lips and she reached up, locked onto him, seeking and delving the space of his mouth.

Goddess, she was passionate!

Her hands gripped harder, trying to push him deeper.

Wrapping his arms around her, he pulled her up as he sat back on his haunches and she sank down his length to the hilt. He nearly lost control as she moaned his name, her body going rigid in his embrace, her breath quick against his mouth. She gripped him. He remained very still, his hands locked her hips in place as she stared wide-eyed into his face, riding and grinding. His thumb grazed her nub and she exploded around him. A moment later he joined her, sparks flaring through his brain as he unloaded.

They remained as they were, skin slick, panting into each other's faces for a long moment. His lips touched hers slowly, softly, then he lay her back upon the pillow, slowly withdrawing. The cool air rushed between them, and he wanted nothing more than to have his body touching hers again.

Retreating to the bathroom, he discarded the spent condom, wiped himself down, then returned with a fresh cloth to clean Lirikai's sensitive flesh.

Her eyes widened in surprise as she watched him do this, trying to take the cloth from his hand to do it herself. Withholding it from her reach, he finished his task, kissed her thigh, and returned it to the bathroom before settling into the bed next to her. Pulling the sheet across their bodies, he pulled her close, tucked her hair into a safe crook and kissed the top of her head.

She said nothing, but entwined her fingers in his before relaxing into sleep. As soon as he heard her breathing shift, he let himself fall to darkness.

ELEVEN

LIRIKAI WOKE TO THE low sound of Carson's voice as he spoke to someone she couldn't see.

Every muscle was relaxed and alive at once. She rolled over, stretching every inch of herself.

She smiled, recalling the night before. Had it all been a wonderful dream? The lack of clothing and the feel of her muscles told her otherwise.

Seated on the arm of the sofa with his back to her and long legs stretched out before him, he held his cell phone device to his ear, listening. He had put shorts on but was otherwise unclothed. She admired his broad shoulders and the strong planes of his back that tapered to narrow hips. The sun was a golden spotlight illuminating his bronzed skin, making all the tiny hairs on his legs and arms glow, as were the tips of his hair, casting him with the halo around his head which she recalled artists favoring at one time.

He lowered his hand, pressing his thumb to the device, and placed it on the desk. Carson scrubbed a hand over his face, and his shoulders rose and fell with a deep sigh as he stood to look out the filmy window.

"What is it?" she asked, sitting up in the bed, chest tight.

He turned at the sound of her voice. "I didn't mean to wake you."

"The sun is up," she shrugged, "What has happened?"

"There's another body. A cop this time."

"A cop? Like... you?"

He nodded.

Her stomach dropped. "Was he a good man?"

It was his turn to shrug, "Woman. Couldn't say, I don't know the cops here very well. Ana might know her. But this changes things. A lot."

Pulling the sheet around herself, Lirikai moved across the room to stand next to Carson. The window was a mix of ocean and city. The sea and beach filled one side, bordered by the coastal highway holding the city back from the water on the opposite side. She looked up at him, waiting.

"With a cop dead, this will motivate the force to find the killer. That means everyone will be working the case, not just me and Ana—and you. That many more people with *hard* motivation."

She swallowed hard. Angry villagers made for brutal messy justice. And these weren't average villagers, they had power and weapons.

Lirikai crossed back to the bed, retrieving the spilled clothing from the floor, looking for something to wear.

"I will find her."

"Lirikai, when we find her, I have to bring her in."

She kept her back to him, lips pressed together.

"Lirikai?"

When she didn't answer, she heard him cross the carpet before his warm hands came to rest on her arms.

She stopped moving for a long moment finding comfort in the touch.

Her sister—she was sure these were the actions of a sister—was in trouble and she had to try to help her.

"I will find her," she said again.

"How?"

Stepping away from those strong hands, she resumed her search through the clothing, growled, and slammed the clothing back onto the bed, "Is there nothing reasonable in this pile?"

"I can take you shopping for new clothes," Carson said.

"There is no time for that," she snapped, snatching undergarments and a blouse.

Carson reached into the pile, "Try these jeans."

With a huff, she grabbed the clothing from his hand and went into the lavatory.

'How?' he'd asked her.

Indeed. The bodies barely had trace scents of anything on them. Normally, she would be able to detect at least a little bit, the scent of the killer, which would guide her in the direction she needed to go. She would not have been working alone to cover a village.

How?

Maybe this new body will lead her in the right direction. Barra'kidai didn't kill innocents or law enforcers. It was against the natural law for what they were created to do. Either this sister had fallen to madness or these victims were corrupt in some way. Abuse of power and position was as old as time. Surely Carson understood that? Or was he too ingrained in the modern world and ideas? Did they not believe such things could happen?

When she emerged from the bathroom, Carson had dressed and straightened the room.

She slid her feet into his flip flops. "I'm ready."

LIRIKAI WAS SILENT WHILE Carson drove them to the scene, which turned out to be close to the restaurant they'd dined at the night before. And now with the body this close to a location they'd just been to, Carson was on alert. It couldn't be a coincidence, could it?

The forensics tent was set up just beyond the rocky outcrop where they'd stashed their clothes. He glanced at Lirikai's face, her brow deeply furrowed and lips tight as she pulled on the white suit. Her nostrils twitched as she turned her head away from the tent scanning the landscape opposite the ocean. Still she didn't say anything but followed him inside.

The body was marked the same as the others, devoid of any identifiers including clothing. She'd been identified by the first responders as a known local officer. Preliminary report in hand, Carson leaned to see the victim's face. Dread clawed through his gut. He'd seen this cop in the bullpen every day. They hadn't been friendly, but she was still familiar.

"Has her family been notified?" he asked Lana O'Brien.

Lirikai crouched, removed her mask leaning to within inches of the body, inspecting the markings.

"Not yet," Lana's face was tight. "We're going to get the son of a bitch that's doing this. No one can take down a cop and get away with it. I've seen too many of these victims. This is someone with no humanity. They need to be put down like a rabid animal."

Lirikai rose from the body and left the tent.

"I need access to any cases she was working. Maybe it's connected."

Lana gave him a sharp nod, "I'll see what I can do."

"We'll need to talk to everyone she worked closely with, and her family," he said, handing the report back to Lana. "Send it to my office as soon as possible."

Lost in thought, he pulled the suit off and discarded it with the others, then turned, expecting to find Lirikai by the shore waiting for him. Not seeing her, he turned again, his gaze sliding over the investigators and again not finding her. Not until he turned his attention up to the parking lot atop the rise did he see her talking to someone in a car.

It wasn't Ana's car. Who else would she be talking to? He called out, walking toward her.

She turned at the sound of his voice, and he could see a woman behind the wheel who spoke to Lirikai. His heart stopped when she darted around the vehicle and got in the passenger side. The car sped off with the door barely closed.

Carson launched into a run for his jeep, parked farther away.

Pulling his cell from his pocket as he ran, he called Ana, relaying what had just happened. Jumping into the jeep, he snapped the cell into its brace on his dash and tore out of the lot in pursuit. His knuckles were white on the wheel as he steered the jeep after the car. At the road, trying to see which direction it went, he listened for the sound of an accelerating vehicle. There was too much traffic on this Saturday afternoon, everyone out enjoying the day of beach and shopping. Far up the road he spotted what he thought was the unremarkable car he'd seen Liri get into and hit the gas, cutting several cars off as he went.

Ana was still on the line, shouting at him to be careful when horns sounded. "I need to get close enough for the plate," he snapped.

"Well don't kill yourself in the process, dammit!"

Carson snarled, "Not helpful." He veered in and out of traffic, eliciting more horns and angry shouts. He didn't have the benefit of a police car's light and sirens to alert people that he wasn't just a random maniac but was a man with a mission.

His heart was pounding in his ears, but it wasn't out of fear of the traffic.

What if Lirikai were hurt? What if he never saw her again? He had to get to her.

But she'd run to get into the car when she heard him. Surely, she wasn't in danger?

What if she was being coerced?

Who was the woman?

Was she a Barra'kidai? Was she THE Barra'kidai?

Was she the killer?

And if she was? What would Liri do?

Would she stop her, or help her?

Would Liri help her sister complete her 'duty' by killing more people?

His foot pressed the gas pedal a little harder.

He had to stop both of them. Where the fuck was the car? He couldn't see it - wait! There it was! It made a right turn at a busy intersection. Carson sped up and darted around the cars blocking his way, thankful for the break in traffic, and continued to tear up the street in time to see it swerve through a narrow gap as the light turned red. He had no choice but to stop hard as a bus suddenly filled the space, lurching, then crawling. Hitting the horn and cursing, passengers peered down at him through the bus's windows confused by his urgency.

As soon as the rear of the bus cleared the front of his jeep, he edged forward but was again cut off by more encroaching traffic. He glanced ahead, frustrated to realize the car had disappeared. He had no idea which way it went. By the time he was able to get through the clogged intersection and up the road, they were long gone.

Ana was still on the line suffering through all the noise, his curses and extreme road rage. "Did you at least get a look at her?"

"Barely," he said as he accelerated up the road, hoping beyond hope to get a glimpse of something, a clue as to which way they'd gone only to discover absolutely nothing.

"Carson, just come to the station, maybe she'll turn up, you never know."

"I will, soon." He said, disconnecting the call.

Instead of turning back toward the office, he pulled over to recall the moments before Liri ran off. Reaching for the glove box, he pulled out a notebook and pen, bulleting the events.

Called to the scene, checked the body. Lirikai had looked at the body and left quickly. Then she was up at the parking lot.

She must have found something on the body to draw her outside. Had she seen something outside before going in? What was she doing before hand? She was looking at the ocean. Had there been someone there?

If this was a Barra'kidai, why would they be lurking around? What were they looking for? How could they know Liri would be there? Was it on purpose? What was going on?

Was Lirikai responsible in some way after all? Had he been wrong about her?

For a second, he thought maybe she had done it herself, but that was ridiculous. They'd been together nearly unbroken since he'd found her on the beach. She wouldn't have had the opportunity to do this last murder. But what of the others? Were they working together? Was her time with him a ruse to get information about the investigation from the inside? Was she playing him? Was she? All this time?

He thought back to their lovemaking. She'd led him away from the parking lot. She'd lured him into the ocean. Maybe it was all a ruse. All of it. She'd lured him out to see what manner of beast he was to see what she was working against.

He'd been so stupid. He'd brought her in on the investigation right away, without any thought as to whether she was involved. That wasn't entirely true, he'd had some thought, but had instantly brushed it a way. Now he had his doubts. He slammed his hands on the steering wheel. How fucking stupid could he be?

He'd never ever been so fucking careless in his life. He'd always been careful about who he let get close to him, and his work had always, always been performed with care.

He'd slipped and wasted time screwing someone who should be suspect. And now a cop was dead.

He thought back over the last day.

How had she found him? How had she known to target him?

"Goddess." She'd said to him when they met.

How could she have known?

She'd sensed it when he'd been swimming in the water. She must have. He could feel the Goddess energy coming from her too.

He dropped his head into his hands, scrubbing them over his face.

He'd instantly let his guard down because of the Goddess.

His natural suspicion had been overridden by his sense of loyalty to the goddess and excitement to meet someone else connected to her.

He'd thought that after all this time, the Goddess had sent someone to help him. Meeting anyone else of the Goddess in his entire long life had been rare occurrence and always had been meaningful. He'd trusted in that.

Had Lirikai helped him at all, or had he just stupidly fed her everything he knew, like a naive child?

He was so angry, he couldn't remember anything but her beautiful face and curvy body. It was all that had filled his mind and senses when they'd been anywhere near each other.

The sense of betrayal and his own stupidity were burrowing deeper and deeper.

This was why he was alone. This is exactly why he kept himself apart from any potential bonds. They either made him weak and got him killed, or they made him weak and got him stupid.

Goddessdammit. As soon as he was done this case, he was going home to his islands. He spent too much time working for the GPSA and needed a break to re-balance himself.

He drummed the steering wheel for a moment, then made his decision. He drew in a deep breath, trying to dispel his anger and find focus.

It had been such a long time since he'd lost himself to anger like that. It was entirely out of character for him to give into such deep and quick rage and doubt.

But as it abated, he felt as though some clarity were settling in its place. Like he'd been burned clean of something that had settled in him, stagnant and filmy. He didn't have a name for what it was just yet, but it would come.

He stared the jeep, made a U-turn on the quiet street and drove back to the scene at the beach.

He was going to go over everything. Everything. Very carefully.

LIRI'S EYES WERE GLUED to the driver's face, still disbelieving. She could not believe who she'd found out by the beach, in a car watching the scene. She had approached the car. Then Carson had shouted for her, and she hadn't thought anymore, just ran to get into the car before she disappeared, and she'd taken it as a cue to escape.

Now, the woman drove carefully, constantly checking the mirrors to see if they were still being followed.

"I can't see him anymore," Lirikai told her in the old language.

They drove on awhile longer. Lirikai's gut was tight over leaving Carson. She'd seen him run after her, then his jeep in the distance following them. She could only imagine what he was thinking right now.

The woman remained silent.

How long? How long had it been since they'd seen each other? But she knew her. She would never forget this face. She never forgot any of her sister's faces. Despite the sallowness of her skin, the sharp bones and haunted look around her eyes. She knew her.

"Milakai, what is happening?"

She steered the car into a diner parking lot that Lirikai recognized. She'd been here with Carson. A shiver slid up her neck.

Her voice was a hard whisper, "Liri, I need your help."

"How did you know I was here?"

"I saw you the other night. I've-I've been following."

"Why?"

"I don't know," her lips opened and closed, her eyes filled with tears. "I don't know," her voice broke.

Lirikai had never seen a sister like this. This was a stranger, not the woman she'd known before.

"Tell me what you've done," she said, her voice soft, her hand reaching out.

Milakai straightened at that, shoulders back, lips settling into a firm line. "I've been doing my duty." The haunted look vanished and her eyes burned with conviction.

Lirikai dropped her hand back to her lap. "What I have seen is not the way of the Barra'kidai, Mila."

"I am Barra'kidai."

"Are you?" she challenged. "The last time I saw you, you were happily waving those of few of us left goodbye while you sailed away with your mate to live a human life. Not a Barra'kidai life."

Mila's head snapped toward Liri, eyes narrowed. "Well, I can no longer live a human life. I need you and the other sisters to help me."

"Mila, there are no other sisters."

Liri watched the emotions play over Mila's face. Shock, pain, resolve. Her voice softened a little. "Then I need your help, Liri."

"What for?" She already knew the answer, but she asked anyway.

"To kill the last one."

"I will not commit murder, Mila, not even for you."

"It isn't murder, it's justice," she snapped.

Her gut flipped over. She'd seen the bodies. And she could see the pain and madness in Mila's eyes. Her instinct was what she always knew—the Barra'kidai were the Goddess' deliverers of justice. But Mila's countenance and surety wormed doubt and fear into her heart.

Never before had she ever doubted a sister, or the purpose of the Barra'kidai. Never.

She hedged, "The last victim was a law enforcer."

"She was complicit," she hissed.

The sound slid up Lirikai's spine. The unnatural tenor and energy rolling off the woman struck her. She could feel the wrongness. The brokenness of her sister.

Was this what happened when the immortal lived too long among the humans?

Would this be her fate too? She'd gone into hibernation because she was tired of drifting alone in the world. The Barra'kidai either found their justice and lived out life as humans or died achieving it for others.

Clearly something had gone wrong for Mila. Centuries later, she was still living among the humans but now she was broken.

"Come to the sea with me."

Liri watched Mila crumble, "I can't! I can't, Liri. I want nothing more than to let the sea take my pain, but I can't."

Mila's grief flooded the small space of the car and Liri was consumed by it and for the first time in millennia was overwhelmed by raw emotion.

Not since the day she looked on the pale life-less faces of her family did she feel such deep grief. It was Mila's, amplified by what little God-dess energy she had left in her, which Liri could feel. It was like a tsunami crashing uncontrolled through the car.

Liri understood this kind of loss. She grabbed Mila's hand. "You're not alone, sister."

Mila bent until her forehead rested on their hands as she cried. Liri waited, tears streaming down her own face unable to stem the flow.

"Tell me of your life since we last saw each other, Mila."

Mila sipped her coffee and Liri waited while she gathered centuries' worth of memories.

"Start with your mate," she prompted, "the reason you left us."

A pang of guilt and sadness fluttered across Mila's face.

"The bond is stronger than anything. It's stronger than what you had with your human family before the Barra'kidai. It's stronger than the Barra'kidai. It's your second chance at a life and it's your call to live that life as fully as pos-sible."

"I thought you'd have died of old age long ago, how are you still here?"

Mila shrugged, "Well, we—John and I aren't sure, but we think it could be because we weren't able to conceive. My body didn't fully change back to human through the influx of hormones that having a child brings to complete the change. And John, well John is special in his own right. He isn't human and lives longer than most anyway." She sipped her coffee again, her eyes tearing up, "We were happy, for so long, Liri."

Liri reached out to squeeze her sister's hand, "What happened Mila?"

"John was investigating a story."

"He's a law enforcer?" Lirikai frowned.

Mila shook her head, "No, not quite. An investigative journalist. He finds out the truth of a situation and shares it with the public, so everyone knows what's going on."

"That sounds dangerous for someone that is not a law enforcer."

Mila shrugged, "He could handle himself. Most of the time, anyway."

"What was his story?"

"I didn't know at first. He was always working on something, and often it was dangerous.

He usually did dangerous. Often, he shared his investigations with me, but I'd been swamped with my own work lately." Her hands tightened on her mug. She took a shaky breath and went on. "The day he disappeared, he gave me his sim card to hold on to because he was taking his phone in to repair a cracked screen. He didn't trust it wouldn't be copied. I had it in my purse when I went to work. He was going to a shady neighborhood where the guy works for cheap out of a pawn shop. When I came back from work the house was wrecked and his office was torn apart. He never came back."

"What happened next?"

Mila's thumb teased the rim of her mug, "I called the police about the break in, of course. They were familiar with him and questioned me about what he was working on. I didn't know what this case was about, but he was putting in a lot of hours. He didn't come back that night, I called the station again in the morning and they asked me to go in."

She paused to collect herself.

"John was supposed to meet me for dinner after he had his phone repaired. And I was trying not to worry about his absence—sometimes it happens when he's on a case. But by morning I was scared."

Lirikai waited in silence.

Mila looked up at her, "Do you remember the old days, when we'd be in a battle and a group of us would get separated? The waiting after the battle for the others to come swimming slowly back, likely wounded and recovering. And not knowing exactly how badly hurt the survivors were and who might have been lost?"

Liri nodded. She remembered.

"It was like that, but the waiting went on. When I went into the station, the officer that came to talk to me asked me a lot about John's work again, and then started asking about our relationship, pushing the questioning in a direction that didn't make sense. She started asking about affairs and maybe he'd just left me for another lover and elaborately tried to make it look like something else. Her dismissive attitude didn't make sense."

"Obviously you couldn't tell her that you and John had been mated for centuries and that your relationship didn't work that way."

Mila nodded. "But her attitude seemed like more was going on than her just being an ass-hole cop patronizing a jilted wife. My instincts, the Barra'kidai instincts, began to resurface in conjunction with my own natural instincts, I knew something was very wrong. Just like that, the Barra'kidai resurfaced under my skin, and I had to get out of there and out to my car before I lost control. It was happening so fast."

Lirikai knew the power of the instinct and how sometimes it was difficult to control. She couldn't imagine what it must have felt like to have had it buried for so long than suddenly break free like that. The utter loss of control would have been terrifying. She'd suspected something like this might have been happening, but now Mila was confirming it in her own words.

"I managed to calm down enough to drive to the beach front. I tried to do a controlled shift. I couldn't do it." Mila's eyes were full of tears. "I couldn't shift entirely, and I was barely controlling the instincts. I was shifting just enough to be dangerous, just a partial, and when it happened the Barra'kidai was in control."

Liri swallowed the horror in her heart. It was one thing to give in to the Barra'kidai in battle, it was another to be ruled by it when you didn't wish to be. A state of nightmare, a nightmare she feared for herself-being ruled by the beast rather than co-existence with it. "Do you think the Barra'kidai will fade once we find your John?"

"I don't know, Liri. If he hasn't come back to me by now, I don't think he will. I'm afraid what will happen when I know for sure he won't. I can't survive that again. Not again. Either I save him, or I die with him."

Liri blinked away her own tears. After all this time, she finally wasn't alone again, only to learn she might very well lose her sister, knowing she will never ever come back. Before, she had thought she might be the last of her kind, but there was still hope. This time, if Mila didn't find John alive, Liri knew she would be the last.

She took a deep breath, "How can I help you?"

The relief in Mila's face was palpable as tears dropping onto the paper covering the table. "When I remembered I had John's sim card in my purse, I put it in my phone and found his notes, which led me back along his investigative trail. I started at the pawn shop where he went to get his phone repaired. He was just the beginning."

Liri watched Mila's eyes turn silver as the Barra'kidai rose to the surface during the retelling of her own investigation to her mate's disappearance. She shivered. It was like the old days. The thrill of tracking and hunting, seeking justice. But Lirikai could also see something else in Mila, a burning that verged on frenzy. An imbalance. Danger.

She accounted for each of the victims in Carson's files. There was no longer any doubt that Mila was killing these individuals. But aside from her mate's disappearance, what were their crimes? Were their deaths warranted? If they weren't then Mila's actions were abominable, making her no better than the criminals the Barra'kidai executed. If she was destroying these people only to assuage the fear of losing her mate, and not because they were guilty of committing terrible crimes, then Mila would have to be destroyed and given over to the goddess.

She felt punched in the chest as she looked at the face of a sister, one she hadn't seen in half a millennia. Was there a chance all this could end well for all of them? What would Carson do if he caught Mila, now that Liri knew she had indeed killed these people.

He would lock her away. Liri couldn't imagine life locked away - especially in a place that housed criminals of the worst sort. She would lose completely to the Barra'kidai under such circumstances and exist in a place of madness.

She couldn't let that happen to Mila. They'd either find John alive and they would go away never to be found, or Mila would die.

TWELVE

ANA SAW CARSON IN his office staring at the files, with their key information displayed on the desktop, trying to piece together the victims' identities.

A cop, an informant, a local spiritual leader and a petty criminal.

A light tap on the door drew his attention. Ana stepped into the room and closed the door when he turned to her.

She approached, staring at the accumulation of photos, her gaze landing on the latest victim.

"I saw her everyday that I've been here," Carson said. "Did you know her?"

She frowned at the photo. "Dana Keenan. A little, but not really. I keep my distance from most of the cops here. I work from this post; I'm not one of them."

He turned toward her so he could see her face, "Why not? You've been here a long time."

She shrugged, "They know I'm not a cop. As a liaison for the federal bureau, they're leery of my presence. But this is the first case that has had us dealing directly. Usually I'm sending agents elsewhere up and down the coast, so I'm ignored." She paused for a moment, pushing the corner of Keenan's photo to straighten it. "I haven't interfered in their business before now. I'm no longer just occupying space, and the dynamic has shifted a bit."

Carson studied the photos a bit longer, not seeing anything new. Not seeing anything at all.

The door to Carson's office slammed open, the precinct captain stood framed in the doorway. Several officers stood behind him. The bullpen was quiet. "You." He pointed at Carson. "Hand over all your work to my men, I want this killer found now."

"This is a federal investigation, captain."

"I don't give a shit. The bodies have been piling up while you're running around doing nothing. One of *my* cops is dead. We'll deal with the problem ourselves."

"It doesn't work that way." Carson turned toward the captain, his voice even.

The captain drew himself up, stomping toward Carson. "Who the hell do you think you are? This is my town, my cops, my territory. You know nothing about how things are run here. Hand over your files and go back to D.C."

Ana's skin prickled when Carson didn't move. The captain stepped to within inches of him. Her breath caught as the energy in the room shifted. Carson didn't move, but he seemed to grow larger, his presence filled the room. Still he didn't move.

The captain took a step back, perspiration sheening his temples, his face going pale.

"Agent Analiese Ortega and I will continue our investigation, Captain Mack. We thank you for your hospitality in your precinct and we will finish our job. We will find out who is responsible for all the tragedy. Then, and only then, will we think about returning to D.C."

Ana watched the captain struggle to contain himself, but after a moment he gave a curt nod, then turned on his heel and walked out. The other officers eventually turned away and the low usual din in the bullpen resumed.

She walked past Carson, closing the door with a soft click, then turned to him and let out a breath. His gaze was still on the doorway. She glanced behind her to see that he was still watching the captain, who was now talking to a couple of his subordinates, off to the side of the room. Every few seconds he'd glance at Carson's office door.

She shrugged, "Like I said, we're not one of them."

"No, we're not," he answered quietly.

"Come on, let's go over the victim's profiles again. Maybe something will pop."

Finally, he nodded and turned back to the task at hand. "I've read over everything, all of the interview reports. I think we'll have to go back and do them again ourselves."

Ana blew out a breath. "Okay." Shuffling through the folders, she pulled free the first one. "First victim, local petty thug, runs a pawn shop in the less desirable end of town. Cause of death blunt force trauma followed by blood loss from the bite marks. The symbol carved into his head was done post-mortem."

Carson nodded.

"Second victim was a spiritual leader of a small congregation in the community, third was an informant, and then Keenan."

"All same M.O."

Ana stepped back a moment, arms crossed, lower lip between her fingers as she considered what was before them. "What feedback has Lirikai given, if any?

"If we can rely on the idea that the killings have been done by a Barra'kidai, which are supposed to be all extinct, with the exception of Lirikai, then legends are that the Barra'kidai maul their victims to death because they are corrupted humans preying on others. They can sniff out the corrupt, which incites the instinct to devour and obliterate them at the behest of the Goddess."

"You know, it doesn't sound any better than the last time we discussed the details."

Carson laughed. "Yeah, no shit."

"So, if we're running with the legend, then every one of these victims is corrupt in some way... including Keenan." Ana said, her glance flickering toward the bullpen beyond the door. She repeated the list, "A cop, a church leader, an informant and a petty thug. Are they linked together, or are they just random?"

Carson turned back toward Ana, "Keenan's body was found very close to an area that Lirikai and I had been the night before.

"Shit." Ana turned back toward the bullpen now, the captain nowhere in sight. "Surveillance? If so, that might make you and Lirikai look suspicious depending on how many in the precinct were aware of this."

"I doubt they'd try to pin anything on me, but they might go after Lirikai."

"Where was she when she wasn't with you that night?"

"She was with me all night. We've been together constantly since she found me on the beach. Except when she was with you...."

"Well now," Ana grinned at him, watching the tips of his ears turn pink. "I guess all that lacy underwear did the trick."

He rolled his eyes at her, but turned away deliberately, focusing on tidying up the files. "Let's go knock on some doors already knocked on."

"Sure, let me get my jacket," Ana said, leaving him to clear up his desk. As she walked through the bullpen to her office, the usual din dropped, and she could feel eyes crawling over her. Suspicion rode high in the atmosphere. Something tugged at the back of her mind, feeling the urge to go and talk to the captain. Veering toward his door, she found him in conversation with the same few officers he'd been chatting with earlier on. He looked up at her approach and the hostility rolled toward her.

"Captain, I just wanted to express my condolences. I know Keenan worked here a long time. I'm sorry."

His jaw tightened, his eyes hard as he stared down at her. Underlying grief spiked the hostility, laced with guilt. "She was a good cop." His jaw worked, looking for proper, professional words to relay.

"I'm sorry I didn't know her better."

"Yeah, well...."

She sensed his impatience for her departure, so she left the group to get her jacket as intended. She found Carson by his jeep waiting for her to get in.

LIRIKAI AND MILA PULLED up to the bluffs overlooking the ocean. "Each of the guilty came out to the beaches for some reason. I tracked them to places relatively near here. John thought they were smuggling drugs to the caves to and from cargo ships."

The late evening winds buffeted their clothes and hair from where they stood looking down the cliff faces. They dropped at the sound of an engine, as a speed boat rounded the light-house point. Engine cut, it drifted, letting the water push it closer to land. It restarted its engine at a barely audible speed, trundling toward where Mila said the cave mouth was.

"Only sea access?" she asked Mila, who nodded. "I'm going in."

"Be careful Liri. I've had to fight my way out of every encounter with those guys."

Lirikai nodded, squeezed Mila's arm and scuttled her way down to an overhang where she stripped and let herself drop into the ocean.

The sea welcomed her as soon as she shifted into Barra'kidai, immediately darting toward the caves.

Staying well below the surface of the water, she swam along the ocean floor, guided by the changes of surf and darkness. Soon, the water level shallowed out and she drifted below the hulls of several speed boats. Shifting back into human form, she surfaced without a sound, careful to use the boats as shields between herself and where she thought the criminals would be lurking. The cave wasn't unlike the underwater cave she'd spend the last few centuries sleeping in. She listened hard, hearing some voices echo off the cave walls, but they didn't appear to be in the immediate chamber. The dim light of the setting sun allowed her just enough light to see that she was alone in the cave mouth. There were three boats tied to large rocks, but she couldn't be sure how many of the enemy would be here, or what she would find. Mila expected she would find barrels or some other kind of containers that would hold drugs or some other contraband.

Creeping up out of the water, she moved as silently on land as she did in the water following the scent of criminals. Keeping to the shadows, she edged farther, and farther still into the cave, listening to the murmur of voices as well as for any noise coming from the direction she'd emerged from. Light splashed the walls as she rounded a corner and she was careful to remain out of sight.

Edging forward, she moved around the bend of the jagged cave wall, until finally she could see something. There were some waist-high barrels made of metal, painted in muted natural colors. The scents of prey were stronger here, and she knew they were close. There were weapons propped atop some of the barrels and leaning up against the cave wall. A lot of them.

"These numbers look about right," a man's voice echoed toward her followed by the sound of fluttering papers. "We're due to move every-thing out tonight, so keep watch for the sig-nals. We shouldn't have any trouble from the coast guard, they'll be occupied elsewhere on the coast."

The sounds of heavy steps scuffing rock and gravel drifted down the tunnel.

"What about these?" a second voice said, fol-lowed by a thud and a muffled cry.

"Don't damage them," the first voice snapped. "The buyers don't like them bruised. They like doing that themselves. Right of ownership, or some shit like that."

"Yes sir. Are they going with the product, or a separate shipment?"

"They're going last. The drugs first."

She couldn't tell how many of them there were, but the odor drifting to her was over-whelming, more so than when she passed through the bullpen at the precinct. Too many for her to deal with alone. Barra'kidai were meant to work as a unit, not as lone soldiers. Mila had been very lucky to survive so many encounters on her own, though Lirikai knew how motivated she was to avenge her husband. Such a mission was all consuming and incredi-bly powerful.

There was a low sound, like what she'd heard from Carson's communication device. Another voice spoke, "Sir, they're still tracking the journalist's wife, they think they're close to trapping her this time."

"Good, I don't know what the hell is going on there with that one. Is she traveling with a guard dog or something?"

"Not known."

"What is the lead?"

"She's been seen with the woman that's been working with the feds."

"Shit. I'd better get back to the precinct and find out what they know. They'll be sniffing out harder now that Keenan's been killed."

Lirikai's heart had begun to hammer in her chest at the mention of being close to trapping Mila. She had to get back and warn her.

"Call me when you've got her and get that information out of her. We need to know what she knows and if we can shut down any possibility of exposure. If she survives the interrogation, ship her out with the others. We'll get our money's worth out of her for all the time and manpower she's lost us."

His voice was rapidly becoming louder.

Lirikai padded back down the cave corridor toward the water, gasping reflexively when her barefoot landed on a sharp rock.

"What the fuck was that?" the voice boomed, feet trampling the ground behind her. "Someone's here, find them" he barked.

Lirikai held her breath, running harder for the shadows of the inlet and dove into the water, no longer holding out on stealth but speed. She shifted immediately, continuing her dive down to the ocean floor and following it as it descended farther out to the ocean. One of the boats roared to life over her head, creating turbulence in the water. She sank lower to avoid the unbearably deafening rumble. Just past the cave mouth its engine cut out, floating on the surface. They were looking for her, waiting for someone that would have to eventually surface for air. Not waiting around for them, she swam back toward the bluffs where she'd left Mila. She shifted and surfaced, then swore. How was she going to get back up? She swam farther along looking for a place to breach the cliffs. Climbing wasn't a skill she had much practice with.

The farther she swam, the harder her heart pounded. She began to pray, as she had not done in many centuries, since the Goddess had abandoned her. She prayed for a break to climb, she prayed for Mila's safety. Finally finding a break, she clumsily launched herself up the rocks, hoping her pale body wasn't noticed against the dark rocky surface. Carefully, to keep an eye on the boat that still floated near the cave mouth, she climbed as quickly as possible while keeping low to the ground. It wasn't easy, and she was leaving more skin behind on the jagged rocks than she thought possible. But her fear kept her going. With some luck, since she didn't think the Goddess was listening, she found her way back to her clothes and shoes, pulling them on over the scraps and gouges in her flesh. Manoeuvring back up the last distance to where Lirikai had left Mila, she could hear scuffling and Mila's shouts as she fought.

Lirikai clawed the rocks to climb faster, only to find Mila snarling and surrounded by armed men, one of whom held her arms tight behind her so she couldn't escape. She swore and spit at them. "If anything happens to me, John's information will go to the media." She struggled, trying to kick at another of the men dodging his way closer to secure her with ropes.

As he launched toward her, her head turned and her eyes widened at the sight of Lirikai preparing to launch herself into the fray, "No!" she yelled shaking her head. "The feds will come for-"   A crack sounded as a weapon hit her and her head dropped.

"Captain thinks she has a guard dog; find it and shoot it."

One of the men broke away as the two others let her drop to the ground to bind her hands.

Lirikai remained where she was, obscured by the rocks and scrub. Everything in her screamed to fight for Mila, but her words had forced a wedge of thought to crack the instinct.

Feds—she meant Carson. Mila had referred to him and Ana as feds during their discussions.

With great effort, she controlled the urge to attack the men with weapons pointed at Mila. They pushed her into the back of one of the unremarkable cars and drove away, leaving the other.

"Where the fuck is this dog she's supposed to have?"

"How the hell should I know, quit bitching and just find the fucker so we can go."

Lirikai considered options.

The wind was still buffeting the cliff, and now and then the scent of criminal whipped past her nose, caused her mouth to water.

They were hunting a dog, and they would find her. If she tried to get back down the cliff, she risked being seen now they were no longer distracted by Mila. They were both armed.

Remaining where she was, she waited for opportunity to present itself.

Maybe, just maybe, the Goddess still watched over her priestesses. Maybe.

Forcing herself to breathe, she waited.

Boots kicked gravel toward her.

She scrambled back down to the ledge and got comfortable.

Rocks skittered down around her. Curses were snatched away on the wind.

"Hey, who the hell are you?"

Looking over her shoulder, a man held a gun not quite aimed at her. One foot planted on a rock, the other on higher ground balancing himself.

She turned, cupping a hand around her ear, indicating she couldn't hear him. The wind blew his scent right into her face and she closed her eyes against the urges overwhelming her control.

He moved closer to her, a lone woman sitting on an ocean ledge watching the sea.

"What are you doing here?" His foot was planted on the loose rock beside her. The scent was all around her now, her teeth were descending.

Carson's voice in her mind interrupted the instinct. With a sigh, she reached up to grab the man's thigh. Startled, he looked down at her hand. He jerked when he looked into her eyes. Tightening her grip, she pulled him down in front of her while launching herself backward into the rising ground.

He flew over her head, screaming, into a heavy splash as he hit the ocean. She didn't know if he survived. She didn't care.

"Carl! Did you find that dog?"

Would it work twice? She guessed not and began to climb.

His reaction to her presence was much like the first guy's, and he smelled just as delicious. More so.

"What are you doing out here, you some kind of hooker? Where's Carl?"

She shrugged, "Nice night."

"Where's Carl?" he repeated. He hadn't pointed the gun at her yet, but his eyes were all over her breasts.

She waved a hand in the direction she'd climbed from.

A cursory glance didn't produce Carl.

She sauntered right up to him, letting her gaze drift to the gun in his hand. A grin broke his plain face. "Gimme some head and I'll let you keep yours."

Lirikai reached out her empty hands, her fingers curling around his belt buckle, working to open it as she stepped into his space, letting her nose graze his throat, inhaling deeply. Mmm yes, this one has done many, many terrible things to those weaker than himself. He was ripe.

"Hurry up." His hand shifted to her shoulder to push her to her knees, but she was faster. Her free hand gripped the back of his neck, pulling his throat into her face and she gave into the Barra'kidai. He gurgled as she spit his adam's apple to the ground. The gun dropped as he reached for his throat, eyes wide. Stepping around him, she shoved him hard enough to send him rolling down the slope toward the cliff. She listened to the thuds and sliding rocks, waiting for the splash that came a moment later.

She smiled, licking her lips.

Just a little taste.

Her Barra'kidai purred.

Retrieving the gun, she went to Milakai's car, got in and stared at the steering wheel.

Now what?

Surely it couldn't be harder than guiding horses pulling a cart?

THIRTEEN

CARSON AND ANA SPENT hours retracing the work of local officers, conducting their own interviews with victim's families and acquaintances. It would take days to cover everyone, of course, but they'd hit up a few of the ones they thought were key to begin with.

Exhausted, he dropped his keys on the hotel room dresser, then threw his notebook on the desk and removed the brace holding his firearm. Dropping into the chair, his gaze fell to the bed. The pile of clothes left by Lirikai had been neatly folded and stacked atop the freshly made bed. He had to remember to leave housekeeping a good tip. His mind drifted back to Lirikai as his eyes remained fixed on the clothing. Lace peeked out among satin folds.

Ana had set him up; she'd read him, and probably Lirikai. But why would she bother getting involved to nudge things along? He didn't do relationships. Not anymore. Immortality had its drawbacks. He scrubbed his hands over his face, trying to clear himself of encroaching memories of the past and stop thoughts about Lirikai and the present from invading.

A click resounded from the end of the short hall and the door eased open. Lirikai's dark shape appeared. She stepped into the light, key card in one hand. Unfamiliar car keys dangled from the other. He jumped to his feet when he saw her face. Her eyes were large and silvered, blood smeared much of the lower half of her face and stained her shirt front.

Moving toward her, his hands reached for her arms, "What happened?"

"I don't ever want to drive a car again," she said.

"What? Did you have an accident?" He peered closer, looking for wounds.

"No, not really, maybe a little—there's no time for that. Mila has been taken."

"Mila? The woman you left with?"

She nodded.

"Is she Barra'kidai?"

"Yes."

"Whose blood is this?"

Lirikai's gaze dropped to her shirt front. When she looked back at his face, her expression was defiant. "A bad man's."

Carson pulled her into the bathroom and turned on the sink faucet snatching a facecloth from the rack. Soaking and soaping it up, he moved to clean Lirikai's face, she grabbed it from him, and scrubbed the cloth over her skin, then held it under the water to rinse.

"What happened?"

"They took her husband."

"Did Mila kill those people?"

Lirikai scowled at him, "She's running away from a bad bunch of people because she has information about them that her husband discovered. She was caught and now they want to get that information from her. If she doesn't die, they will sell her."

Carson straightened. "Human trafficking ring. We thought it was drugs."

"They have that too."

"Where was she taken?"

Lirikai told him about their trip out to the cliffs and her venture into the caves.

"You went in there alone?"

"We needed to see."

"And you were nearly captured too," he gestured to her shirt.

She shrugged, "I defended myself."

"What did you do with the bodies?" he prayed she didn't mutilate them, it would make things complicated to try to explain in court.

"Let them roll off the cliff. The sea claimed them."

He took the cloth from her hand, rinsed it again and wiped at a few blood smears she'd missed. "Do you know where they were taking her?"

"I'm not sure. But there are people in that cave, and they're being transported tonight. She might be sent with them if she survives."

"I'll call Ana and tell her to talk to the captain, she went back to the precinct."

Lirikai straightened, "one of the men in the cave said he was going back there to find out what the feds knew-that's you and Ana, yes?"

Carson nodded. Dammit. Cops were involved in this. Pulling his cell from his pocket, he called Ana. "Lirikai is back. Be careful, cops from the precinct are involved in a drug and human trafficking ring. They're running between caves and cargo ships. There's an exchange tonight."

"That would explain the gaps in the reports and shoddy interviews, dammit. Does she know who's on the take?"

"She didn't see any faces."

"Okay," there was a long pause, "The captain just came in to the precinct, I'll go talk to him and call you back shortly."

Carson slid the phone back into his pocket.

Lirikai changed her shirt and was waiting for him. "We have to go back for Mila."

"Do you know that's where they're taking her? We have no guarantee they'll take her there." Something shifted in Carson's memory. "Who was Mila's husband?"

"She said he was a journalist. Ehm.. John Welsh."

"Shit, there's a warrant out for her. She's wanted on suspicion of his death."

"She didn't kill him."

He nodded, "They're after his information? They'll interrogate her."

"Yes, and if they don't kill her, they'll send her away with the other prisoners."

"Alright, lets head out there while Ana's talking to the captain."

Once they were outside by his jeep, Carson paused to send Ana a text to let her know where they were headed. As he glanced up, he recognized the car Lirikai had taken off in with Mila. It was in rough shape, the sides were scraped, and fenders crumpled, one mirror hung askew.

"I'm going to teach you how to drive when all this is done."

LIRI LED CARSON BACK to the bluffs where Mila was taken. He found an obscured place to leave the jeep, and she waited while he retrieved a few things from the back. From their vantage point, she could see a vast ship drifting down the coast. It was still a long way out, but she knew they wouldn't have much more time.

He appeared next to her holding a net bag with clothing inside. They climbed down to a place close to where Lirikai had gone into the water before. They stripped down, moonlight washing their skin in pale shades. Carson added their clothing to the netted bag. "You said they have weapons in the cave?"

She nodded.

"Plan is to get to their weapons. All else fails, I'll shift if I have to. You stay out of sight and free the prisoners. They are priority above all else."

"Of course."

"Try not to kill anyone."

She frowned at him.

"Self defense is allowed."

She smiled and leapt into the ocean.

An instant later he was next to her, and she swam ahead, leading him to the mouth of the cave. Looking back, he shimmered in the moonlight water, the netted bag hooked by a claw as his lithe body wove him through the ocean along behind her.

She was relieved to see the boats still as they were.

Shifting into human form, she moved to the ledge, where they pulled clothes from the bag, gave them a quick wring out, and pulled them on. Carson wedged the bag into a crevice, and they snuck along the wall. Voices drifted along the rock toward them as they crept forward.

Lirikai peered around the corner to see two armed men talking. "I'm going to the back for a round of poker while we wait," One guard said, checking his watch.

The other nodded. "Let me know if the cards are good tonight."

"They're good every night Joe, you just gotta know how to play them."

Lirikai watched him disappear toward the back of the lit cave then stepped out into Joe's line of view.

"What are you doing here?"

"My boat turned over, can you help me?"

He eyed her a moment. She stepped toward him, moving round him, drawing his focus.

"You can't be in here."

As soon as he'd turned his back enough, Carson snuck behind him and knocked him out, lowering him to the ground and taking his weapon. Farther up the path, most of the weapons Lirikai had seen earlier were still as they were. She grabbed several and ran back to drop them into the water, letting them sink under the boats. She did this several times until there were none left to be used against them in a skirmish.

Ignoring the barrels lining the path, their bare feet made no sound on the cave floor as they moved along to an opening. Peering inside, she saw about a dozen people huddled along the walls in the dim light, their hands and feet bound. There were no guards with them.

"Get them out of here," Carson whispered as continued.

Lirikai darted toward the first victim, evaluating the binds. They were all gagged and unkempt, clearly having been there for many days. Some were dressed for the beach while others looked as though they were dressed for an evening of entertainment. They must have all been taken from areas near the beach front.

"We must be very quiet," she whispered, "We don't have much time to get you out of here." Moving to the first victim, she untied the gag. "Help me free the others, do you know how many guards are here?"

She shook her head, "They come and go, we never see any of them more than two at a time."

Plastic ties secured her wrists and ankles, the flesh cut and scabbed. Relieved they hadn't used chain or some other metal, she considered running back to check the unconscious guard for a knife. Instead, she bent her head low, let her Barra'kidai teeth extend enough to snip the plastic between the powerful points.

The woman gasped and jerked backward on seeing this, "Jesus!"

"Hold still." She commanded, elevating the woman's legs so that she could access her ankles. It was awkward, but the binds dropped away, and the woman scrambled away from Lirikai, eyes wide in the low light. The woman glanced toward the path to escape.

"Help me free the others," she said, her voice hard, "Or you'll wish you'd been sold tonight."

Nodding, she lurched toward a young man bound farther inside the cave, removing his gag.

"Who are you?" his voice was low, but she could hear the strain of fear.

"Help. Federal officers are on their way."

As the gags fell away, whispering began.

"Stay quiet," she demanded, snipping ties with her teeth as quickly as she could. "My friend is farther inside. Don't make any noise to draw them out."

Several of the victims got to their feet, holding onto the walls for support, their limbs weak from too long without movement. Lirikai kept an eye on them as she worked. There were still a few left bound when she stood and moved toward the corridor.

"Help each other. If you don't, some of you will be caught again." She looked into their faces and knew some of them didn't care. Someone was going to make a go of it. As she moved away from the entrance to return to the remaining prisoners, she heard the quick intake of breath as one of the freed ones made her move. But Lirikai was faster. She pivoted, grabbed a handful of hair, and slammed the young woman to the floor. She landed hard, knocking air from her lungs, and she lay dazed.

Lirikai put her hand around the woman's throat, "I told you to wait." She snarled, letting her teeth extend. There were several gasps and she looked up at all of them. "They intend to sell you to buyers that will do whatever they want to you. If you want to go home, help each other, or none of you will."

There were two prisoners left when shouts echoed down the corridor.

Carson.

Returning to her task, she freed the last two helping them to their feet and led them back out. Some were still strong enough to move without issue, but a few of those that had been there longer required support. Several couldn't walk without help.

Gunfire, followed by the sound of growling, and then more gunfire. She resisted the pull toward the back of the cave, trusting that Carson would be able to handle himself, as she helped the prisoners into the three boats. As soon as they were all loaded, the roar of engines filled the cave and Lirikai ran back to help Carson. Gunfire, snarling, and screams filled the cave complex. The narrow passage opened into a cave a great deal larger than the one the prisoners had been kept in. Carson filled most of it and had two gunmen trapped between himself and the rocky wall, guns pointed at him. Several bodies littered the floor. She didn't know if they were alive, and she didn't care.

There were guns pointed at Carson. They were clearly terrified, but held their ground. His scales rippled in the low light and blood streamed in several places.

"I think you've angered him."

Startled by her voice, one turned his gun in her direction, the other glanced but held his own gun on Carson.

"He might let you go if you put your weapons down."

"Fuck you!"

Carson snarled. The gun wavered.

"He just wants to know who you're working for, and I want to know where my sister is, that's all." She could smell their tightly controlled fear, mingled with the scent of their intentions. "You've lost your prisoners, business will be tricky."

"Shoot her," the one aimed at Carson said.

"What makes you think it won't attack us if we do?" she recognized him as the guard talking to other guard, Joe.

"He will."

"What the fuck is it?"

She shrugged, "You should be more concerned with what he wants. As I said," she moved farther into the space and closer to the gun, maintaining eye contact with her would-be killer. "We just want to know who you work for and where my sister is. Then you can go."

CARSON IGNORED THE POINTS of bullet penetration. Most of the spray had been deflected off his scales, but a few managed to slip between. So long as he stayed in his current form, he could hold out longer against blood loss.

Liri ran into the cave, and it was all he could do not to attack the remaining gunman pointing his weapon at her.

He couldn't believe she was actually walking toward the guy, but he held his position as she negotiated. He'd heard the boats leave the cave and was relieved the prisoners were no longer a concern. They'd likely go to the police. Whether there were dirty cops at the precinct, or not, more than a dozen victims couldn't be ignored.

"I don't know who you're talking about" the guard with his gun pointed at Lirikai said. "All the merchandise was in the front cave, go look in there." His eyes were intent on her, challenging her to turn her back on him.

"She wasn't among those escapees," she said stepping closer. "Where else would a captive be taken?"

The guard's hands tightened on his weapon, raising it a fraction so that it aligned with her head.

Carson growled, the low sound reverberating through the space confining him.

The guard jerked, his attention diverted.

Lirikai's hand shot up, slamming the muzzle away from her face. The gun fired.

Distracted, Carson slammed the man in front of him backward, cracking his head into the cave wall, and swung toward the one that shot

Lirikai, snapping his jaws around him. The bad guy screamed as he bit down then released the body.

The air around him shimmered as he began to shift to human form.

"Don't change!" Lirikai shouted, "Your wounds are too severe."

He snorted his displeasure, moving his snout toward her injured shoulder. Blood streamed down her arm.

"I'll heal when I return to the sea. You will too?"

He dipped his head.

Looking for something to staunch the blood flow, she found his shredded clothing nearby and used strips of it to bind over her wound. Her skin was already turning pale. She then used the rags to wipe at some of the blood on his scales and inspect his wounds. "You have to get into the water as soon as possible."

The whine of a boat engine grew louder as it trundled into the outer cave. They could hear the voices of several men as soon as the engine cut.

"Where are the fucking boats?" someone shouted. "Get the barrels loaded."

"The cave is empty, there's no one here."

"Joe's down."

"Shit."

AT THE SOUND OF booted feet running deeper into the cave, Lirikai dropped the fabric and walked out to meet them before they could see Carson in shifted form. Carson tensed, listening.

"What the hell are you doing here?" a familiar voice echoed along the corridor. "Where is Agent Carson Parenga?"

"Officers?" The reek of corruption assaulted her senses in the confined space.

Lirikai's gaze went to the two familiar faces. She'd seen them at the precinct. Ignoring them, she went farther out toward the mouth of the cave to find Mila barely able to stand, bound and bleeding, her arm in the precinct captain's grip.

Her eyes widened and she shook her head, trying to speak behind the gag in her mouth.

Rage rippled through Lirikai's body at the vision of her battered sister.

"Why is she bound?" she forced the words through clenched teeth. Each of the men were carrying pistols.

"She's responsible for all the murders. Crazy bitch has been mutilating them for some cult god or something." He shrugged, "Case solved, you feds can go home."

"Why are you here?" she asked, moving closer.

His eyes fell to the wound and blood staining her arm, "Rounding up accomplices," he said.

"All prisoners are free, accomplices taken out."

His mouth snapped shut, his jaw tight, nostrils flaring. His chest heaved as he controlled his anger.

"Boss?"

"Why don't we go back to the precinct together?" The captain said through gritted teeth. His eyes bored into her.

Mila shook her head, eyes wide.

Lirikai considered her, then looked at the weapon he carried, she turned her attention to the other two officers, also armed.

With pistols, there were too many to take on.

She stepped away from Mila, closer to the captain's opposite side.

"Don't worry, she's cuffed."

"Did you beat her?"

He smirked. "We interrogated her. She was uncooperative."

Her mouth watered as she fought the instinct to bite him.

The captain stopped smirking, stepping back when he saw her eyes.

"She is the widow of a slaughtered journalist."

"Yeah, so?"

"A journalist investigating missing people and corruption along the coast. Law enforcement profiting from smuggling."

"Bullshit."

"There's evidence of your involvement." His hand swung up, pistol pointed at her head.

She sighed. Again. So predictable.

"The evidence, hand it over."

She shrugged and shook her head.

Mila tried to speak through her gag.

He tightened his grip.

"You should let her go," she said.

"Like fuck."

"Boss, she's with the feds."

"She can't tell them anything if she's dead."

"Nor can I tell you where the evidence is if I'm dead. Release her."

His eyes narrowed on her, "you want me to let her go, huh?" he turned to point the gun at Mila's head. "Funny, we couldn't get anything out of her, maybe we can make you talk instead."

Mila shook her head at Lirikai once more, then went very still and closed her eyes, straightening her spine.

"Boss, we don't have time for this shit."

The captain tossed his head, "Move the barrels."

"Drop your weapon before I destroy you." Lirikai's voice was even as she stepped toward him.

The captain laughed, shook his head, and swung the gun back in her direction.

A deep growl rumbled through the cave.

All at once, Mila's teeth erupted, slicing through her gag. She launched toward the captain, her jaws descending on his shoulder. Carson had come running into the cavern, drawing the attention of the other two cops, who scrambled for their weapons and began firing instinctively and shouting.

Knees buckling under the assault, the captain twisted and fired into Mila's abdomen a second before Lirikai launched herself at him. Mila crumpled to the cave floor as Lirikai and the captain crashed into the water. They fought as she rolled them into deeper water, under the blows of his fist as he struggled to get his hands around her throat. Slipping from his grasp, she waded farther into the water. The captain pursued.

"Captain!" one of his men screamed as Carson batted him with a massive clawed paw, sending him bouncing into the cave wall.

Seeing this, Captain Mack moved farther into the water.

Carson moved to the water's edge, taking a menacing step into the water.

The captain turned to swim for the cave mouth only to be confronted by Lirikai, who blocked his escape.

"Move or I'll feed you to it!" The captain's eyes were wild with fear.

She returned his earlier smirk. "He won't eat you, but I will." She said licking her lips.

"What the fuck?"

Her teeth erupted and, as he screamed she grabbed him, dragging him down into the ocean water, twisting deeper. She shifted, circling him as he clumsily tried to lash out at her, hindered by the resistance of the ocean.

Her sleek body enabled her to slide around him with ease, biting and nipping into his flesh, dragging him farther and farther out into the ocean. When the air and resistance went out of his body, she dragged him still. She didn't stop swimming until she reached her cave where she performed the rite of the Barra'kidai.

The last Barra'kidai.

By the time she was done, there was only the skull of the supremely guilty, left for the Goddess of the Ocean, whether she still desired offerings or not. She wouldn't return to the surface with it to inscribe it, it would be left as it was, nameless and forgotten.

FOURTEEN

CARSON STUFFED THE LAST few file folders into the cardboard box. A quick glance around the office ensured that was everything before he slipped his hands into the handles to transfer it to Ana's office.

"Thanks Carson," she said as he dropped it on a nearby chair.

"How's the round-up coming along?"

"We're working with the Coast Guard to retrieve the barrels of contraband and investigate the trafficking ring at sea, as well as here. They obviously have internal unit issues too."

"Everyone escaped alright?"

She nodded, crossing her arms, leaning back against the wall. "Some are in the hospital for dehydration, malnutrition and battery, among other things, the others have gone home after being looked over and discharged. Lana and her crew have been visiting them for interviews."

"They're a good unit."

"Carson, how are you doing?"

He met her gaze, "I'm fine. Healing up."

She walked around her desk to close the office door.

"Are you? I saw how many slugs were dug out of you."

"Yeah thanks for calling in the GPSA medics."

She patted his arm and gave it a light squeeze.

He sighed, moving away from the contact, running his hands over his face. When he turned back to her he smiled, "I have your bag of clothes in my jeep."

She frowned, "Why don't you hang on to them for Lirikai?"

He shook his head, "I don't think she's going to come back."

"She doesn't know about her sister?"

"No."

"Oh, that's a shame. She should know. I'm sure it would make a great difference to her."

"She's been alone for so long-"

"So have you."

He snapped his mouth shut, giving her a baleful look.

"And despite what you keep saying, Carson, you're *not* an island."

"Hey, you're crushing my sense of ego here, Ortega."

Ana went quiet for a long moment. Her eyes glazed over.

"Ana?"

At the sound of her name, she turned her face to Carson, eyes clearing. She went back to open her office door, "I suggest you go out for a swim and speed up the healing process." Ana gave him a smile and a wink.

He studied her face as he approached, but could see nothing but a genuine smile as she waited for him to pass.

"The waves will be good tonight," she said as he passed through the hive of the bullpen.

CARSON REACHED TO PULL his surfboard free from the back of his jeep, catching himself as an electric twinge shot through the muscle near one of the bullet wounds. Catching his breath, he reminded himself not to move so fast, then carefully eased the board up.

He turned toward the ocean, taking a moment for the pain to pass. He watched the waves roll in, break and turn to froth. Board or free swim?

Liri drifted through his thoughts as another wave lapped up the beach sand. Moving down toward the water, he stood to watch the ocean roll for awhile, and his toes sank into the sun-warmed sand.

He had waited at the hotel. There'd been no sign of her. Carson had gone swimming in the ocean after the bullets had been removed from his body so that he could heal faster. There'd been no sign of her anywhere near the cave. He knew she had to be alright. She'd have shifted, and he'd decided not to stop a Barra'kidai doing her duty. The captain wasn't worth interfering for. Early interviews and reports were coming back indicating he'd instigated the traffic ring. He hadn't been coerced or bought. He'd created it using his status and position.

Carson knew that if he hadn't been deeply corrupt, Lirikai wouldn't have taken him. If he hadn't threatened the life of her sister and imprisoned so many people for profit. His own sense of the law didn't hold up his conscience in this case.

The captain drowned trying to escape justice, was the story relayed to the precinct.

The ocean found him and delivered its own kind of justice.

"I didn't think you'd come."

Carson whirled around.

Lirikai stood behind him, the ocean breeze blowing at her hair and dress. After a long moment, he said, "Nice dress."

She smiled crookedly, "I found it."

"Found it, huh?"

She nodded, stepping forward. He could see the uncertainty in her face. He held out a hand to her. She looked down at his proffered hand, her expression turning sad. "I couldn't leave the captain for you."

He dropped his hand, nodding, "I understand."

She studied his face as though she didn't believe him.

"After what he did to Mila-"

"She's missing you."

She jerked, startled by his words, "Missing me?" tears sprang to her eyes and she shuddered. "She's alive?"

Carson's heart broke looking at her, "Yes, Lirikai, she's alive and recovering in the hospital."

Her hand fluttered at her stomach, her whole body sagged with her relief. "Good," she sniffed back her tears, "that is very good."

He watched her transition as despair threatened to return, "Will she be imprisoned?"

"No. In light of all that has happened, the GPSA are taking her in. She's going to work with us."

A smile spread across her face and she inhaled deeply of the sea air.

Carson's heart mended a little.

"Will you?"

"Will I what?"

"Work with us."

She turned back to him, studying his face. He was sure she could read the hope in him. But she turned toward the city scape. "I don't know."

"You wouldn't be alone anymore. Mila is here, you know that now. And I'm here."

He held out his hand again.

She searched his face for a long time. "I...." She swallowed, looking away from him. "In my human life, I could not give my husband children."

He didn't lower his hand.

"I thought you should know that."

He nodded, watching her face closely. His hand didn't waver.

Her gaze rested on that outstretched hand for a long moment before she tentatively reached out. Her fingers drifted across his palm and curled to grasp him.

Looking into her eyes, he lifted their hands to brush his lips over her knuckles before he placed a kiss on the back of her hand.

She smiled at him and his heart completed the mending and swelled a little.

"First thing I'm going to do is teach you how to drive."

She scoffed, "No you're not! I'm going to teach you how to swim!"

"Oh really?" He pulled her against him and kissed her lips until she opened to him. Accepting her invitation, his tongue swept across hers and she moaned.

"Race?"

"Absolutely." He kissed the tip of her nose.

She wriggled out of his embrace and ran for the sea.

He was two steps behind, catching her dress as she pulled it over her head and released it to the wind, laughing.

Enjoyed reading about Carson & Lirikai? Their work continues...

The Global Paranormal Security Agency

JodiKendrick.com

Thank You!

Dear Reader,

Thank you so much for taking the time to read Awakened. If you enjoyed it check out Jod iKendrick.com for more Romance, Adventure and Passion!

Awakened was originally written for Milly Taiden's Federal Paranormal Unit (FPU) world as part of a group project of aquatic themed shifters with other awesome authors. Some of their characters appear in the opening scene and their books are listed on my webpage for Awakened.

I hope you'll check them out!

-Jodi

Jodi Kendrick

Jodi Kendrick lives in Eastern Ontario Canada with her *Favourite Person* and chompy furbaby, while their adult children explore the wider world.

As a romance author, she writes in paranormal, fantasy, steampunk & gaslamp subgenres, and sometimes delves into urban fantasy and paranormal women's fiction. Her characters are often quirky, sometimes cranky, but they all woman-up and get the job done while their partners ensure they survive with all their bits and bobs attached.

A history enthusiast and word dabbler most of her life, she enjoys exploring 'beyond-the-everyday' and the 'time-before-now', discovering relationship threads weaving individuals through time and place. She's rarely seen without flashy notebooks and colourful pens.

Follow Jodi on Social Media:

Dragon Island

Dragon Heat

Enchanted Ardor

Wish

EveL Worlds : FUCN'A

Tough Nut
Diamond in the Ruff
Honeyed Nut
Gorilla in the Hiss
FUCN'A Collection One
Pedigree Collection

Finely Aged

Dragon Steel

Global Paranormal
Security Agency

Awakened
Surfacing
Polestar
Aquatic Investigations
Prowler

The Kindred Chronicles

Healer
Mercenary

The Soaring Dragon Chronicles

Return Flight
Changeling